Pride

Terence Blacker's book
the bestselling *Ms Wiz*
ture, *Nasty Neighbours/.*
Disappearing Hamster.
for adults, *Fixx* and *The Fame Hotel*.

TERENCE BLACKER

HOTSHOTS

Pride and Penalties

A Piper Original
PAN MACMILLAN
CHILDREN'S BOOKS

First published 1994 by Pan Macmillan Children's Books

a division of Pan Macmillan Publishers Limited
Cavaye Place London SW10 9PG
and Basingstoke

Associated companies throughout the world

ISBN 0-330-32912-X

Copyright © Terence Blacker 1994

The right of Terence Blacker to be identified as the
author of this work has been asserted by him in accordance
with the Copyright, Designs and Patents Act 1988.

3 5 7 9 8 6 4

A CIP catalogue record for this book is available from
the British Library

Typeset by CentraCet Limited, Cambridge
Printed by Cox & Wyman Ltd

This book is for:

Jane

Elizabeth

Martha   Candy

Leila

Alice
Beth

St Peter's, Hammersmith, 1990

Meet the Hotshots

We're gathered at the hamburger bar on the High Street for our first meeting since that eventful evening in a police park in July.

The idea is to discuss the future of the team.

Some hope.

"And in his toolbox, he's got this *chainsaw* – "

Tara's telling us (and anyone else within about a hundred yards) about this gross horror movie she's just seen on video. Roberta and Charlie are laughing so much that they spray Coke all over the table. Lisa's arranging her hair and pretending to be above it all. Ellie's inspecting her salad to check for meat contamination. Stevie puffs at her straw like some million-dollar babe waiting for her date in Hollywood.

Jamie winks at me and takes a chip off my plate. "Great team talk, eh?" he says quietly.

"Yeah."

Tara leans forward. "And under his pillow – " she lowers her voice dramatically " – he keeps a rotting human *hand*!"

Stevie takes the straw out of her mouth. "One more

word about this film, Tara," she says, mock serious, "*one* more – and I swear I'll barf all over this table."

"I'm thinking of writing it all down," I say to Jamie.

"Quite a horror story." Jamie's still staring at Tara.

I laugh. "Just another gem from Tara and her nasty collection."

"Eh?" Jamie looks puzzled. "No, I meant the Hotshots story. You should do it though."

"Maybe I will."

CHAPTER ONE

Powderpuff

It's a well-known fact that, by the time they reach their teens, girls are more intelligent, sensitive, adult, aware and generally brilliant than boys.

If you had the slightest doubt about this fact, you should have been in our classroom the day that our headteacher Mr Kenneth Morley breezes in to tell us that Broadhurst Comprehensive is to enter two teams into the Metropolitan Cup (Under 13 Section).

Suddenly it's feeding time at the zoo. The room echoes to the chants and grunting noises that boys use to express pleasure.

"Here we go, here we go – "

"Easee, easee – "

"We're gonna win the cup, we're gonna win the cup – "

"Thank you, lads," says Mr Morley, smiling uneasily like a man not used to being this popular. "I'll be choosing the teams in the usual way."

"Oh, sir" – Jason, tall, strong, the class bruiser, is sitting at his normal desk at the back of the class – "can't you leave it to us to choose the teams?"

"Jason, you know where I stand on this matter," says Mr Morley with a slightly patronizing grin.

"Yeah – in the wrong," Jason mutters. Almost for the first time in history, I have to agree with him.

Ignoring a growing level of chat in the classroom, Mr Morley pulls out a manky little bit of paper from the top pocket of his jacket and, in a brief moment of weakness, I feel sorry for him with his balding head, his hunched shoulders, his ginger moustache drooping apologetically over thin, well-meaning lips. The Head has standards of basic decency. He likes to be fair. Trying to be decent and fair while running Broadhurst Comprehensive must be like collecting for Christian Aid on the streets of Hell.

"My team," he says, raising his voice over the din. "Mark . . . Richard . . . Jonathan . . ."

Sure enough, the team is a carefully selected list of every nerd and malco in the class. Morley's concept of fairness is based on some mushy concept that has nothing to do with talent. I, for example, being the smallest in the class, would probably be selected as high jumper for the school. Jason would be a certainty for a Brain of Britain contest.

"Great team, sir," he's going now, a cocky little grin on his face.

Unfortunately for Mr Morley, even Jason and his gang, who've got about three brain cells between them, have worked out a way around this system. Not that it's difficult, if you happen to be as big and brutal as Jason is. Over the next couple of days, the nerds and malcos will have mysteriously developed ankle problems, or sick grannies that need looking after, or a deep concern for their homework. One by one they'll leave the team, to be replaced by Jason and his chums.

"And the girls – " Mr Morley looks around the class with a sickening, I'm-no-sexist smile. "Well, we have . . ."

What we have is the same sort of team that last year was humiliated 8–0 in the first round of the Under 12 Section of the Met. Then we didn't care; now we do. Pride's at stake.

Lisa raises her hand.

"Mr Morley, sir," she says, "a few of us have been practising football every Tuesday afternoon after school, sir. We were really hoping to represent the school, sir."

People listen to Lisa. She's got all the confidence that height, a pretty face and a talent for sport can bring.

"And what about the girls who haven't been able to take Tuesday afternoon off?" says Mr Morley wearily. "Don't you think they deserve to play some football?"

"But we're good, sir." Lisa runs her fingers through her heavy dark hair as if she can't believe what she's hearing.

"Good?" The Head frowns. "All the more reason to give someone less . . . good a chance."

"Don't worry, sir," Jason pipes up at the back. "They're total rubbish anyway."

Now this, even by Jason's standards of world-class stupidity, is not a brilliant remark. In fact, good old lamebrain Jase has just thrown us a lifeline.

Mr Morley's face turns an odd, mottled colour. "If I hear any more of that sexist rubbish, Jason Roberts," he says, "you'll get a detention."

It's the moment of truth. I put my hand up.

"Yes, Eve?"

"We're always being told that girls are rubbish at football," I say in my most innocent voice. "If you'd only let us pick our own team for the Cup, we could prove them wrong."

There's silence in the class as Mr Morley ponders this astonishingly cunning suggestion. If Lisa or Tara, both of whom look like athletes, had wanted to select a team, he wouldn't have listened. But me – little Eve Simpson with the pasty face and skinny legs – I can be relied on to speak up for nerds everywhere.

"All right, Eve," he says at last. "Who d'you want?"

Without a second's hesitation, I reel off the names of the team. "Ellie, Roberta, Tara, Charlie, Lisa – she's captain – and me."

Mr Morley sighs. "D'you have to have a captain?" he asks. "Can't you just . . . share?"

"We'd prefer a leader," I say.

"Don't follow leaders, you're watching parking meters," he mutters.

"Sorry, sir?" Mr Morley occasionally lapses into weird sixties-speak without bothering to translate for us.

"Just a song, Eve," he mutters wearily. "Just an old man's song. All right, if no one has any objections, I'll agree to that team."

There's silence in the classroom.

"We'll call ourselves the Hotshots," says Ellie – and suddenly it's zoo time again, with all the boys laughing and jeering at us.

"Hotshots?" Jason sneers. "You have got to be kidding."

That boy is in for a big, big surprise.

I can't think of one good reason why Tara Williams and I have ended up as best friends.

She's good at sport and I'm lousy at it. I do okay in class, she's anchored down at the bottom with Jason and the rough boys. She's big, I'm a shrimp. I do ballet, she's into martial arts. She's our star goalkeeper, while I'm one of life's substitutes.

But we like each other. I suppose that's why we're best friends.

"I bet it's going to be different," I say to Tara as we change for football the following Tuesday. "It will be all serious now that we're the official school team."

"Shut up it will be serious." Tara tugs hard at the lace to one of her trainers. It snaps. "*Lame,*" she says as if the lace had broken particularly to annoy her.

I reach into my sports bag and give her my spare lace which, with mumbled thanks, she threads into the trainer. As usual Tara will be last on to the pitch, even with me helping to get her ready.

Soon we're walking out to the playground, me in my new pink T-shirt, Tara towering over me in torn jeans with her wild blonde hair sticking out from under a dirty baseball cap. Talk about the odd couple.

7

"Ooh, watch out, everyone – it's the Hotshots," Carl, one of Jason's friends jeers as we walk past.

Casually, Tara flicks him the finger. "Get a life, loser," she says without even bothering to look at him.

"Neat fashion statement, Tara." Stevie, an American girl who came to Broadhurst this term mutters as she passes us on her way out of school.

"She's just jealous," I say quickly as Tara turns angrily. Shrugging her broad shoulders, she continues on her way to the playground.

But there's a shock in store when we reach the pitch. There, standing in the centre circle, a football under her arm, is Miss Wilson, our geography teacher.

"I don't believe it," says Tara, as the other players gather around. Miss Wilson is not exactly blessed with the right shape for football (sumo wrestling, yes, football, no) and the bright purple tracksuit she's wearing hardly flatters her figure.

"Right, girls," she announces. "I'm your new manager, as from today. What d'you call yourselves? Hot Shoots?"

We look at one another in silent amazement. So much for the Head not liking leaders.

"Hotshots," says Lisa. "Er, Miss Wilson, d'you actually know much about football?"

"I'll have you know I was captain of hockey." Miss Wilson's face dimples at the memory. "It's the same sort of thing. Now who's going to bully off?"

"Bully off?" mutters Tara. "What's she talking about?"

Mumbling moodily, we sort ourselves out. About twelve girls usually turn up for practice games. Some are in the Under 12 team, others enjoy playing football but don't want to take part in competitions. To make it fair, the six members of the Hotshots are split up between each team. As usual Lisa and Ellie are voted captains. As usual, I'm the last to be picked. As usual, no one apart from Tara wants to be in goal. As usual, it ends up being me.

At first we manage to play our normal game, ignoring Miss Wilson as she huffs and puffs up and down the pitch, shouting things like "Nice *ball*, Lisa!", "Control, girls?" and "*Excellent* retrieving!"

Lisa shimmies past most of the other players as if they aren't there. Tara makes some amazing saves. Big, strong, unflappable Charlie is so brilliant in defence that the goalkeeper behind her (guess who?) hardly has to touch the ball, which, to tell the truth, is absolutely fine by her.

In fact, the game's going really well until Roberta decides to deploy the ultimate secret weapon – her left foot.

Roberta's one of those players who seem to be dreaming for most of the time until the moment, once or twice in the game, when she catches sight of goal and decides to let fly. When Roberta gets that look in her eye, the way clears before her and even Tara has been known to duck.

Except this time she doesn't have to. Roberta limbers up, draws back her left foot and –

9

"Miss Wilson!" I yell at the teacher whose back is turned as she tries to shoo some boys away from the wire outside the school. "Watch out!"

Too late.

As Roberta releases a cannonball of a shot, fate guides the ball straight into the small of Miss Wilson's back.

Oooooof! Like a great Californian redwood, she keels over. I could swear that there's a faint earth tremor as she hits the concrete.

For a moment we stand there, unable to believe what we've just seen.

"You are an *animal*, Berta," one of the boys beyond the wire shouts with an uncertain laugh. We run to where Miss Wilson is lying, moaning.

When she turns over, we see that her face has gone the same colour as her tracksuit.

"I'm really sorry, Miss Wilson." Roberta seems on the verge of tears.

"Euurraaagghhhh." The noise coming from the teacher sounds like water gurgling down a vast, cavernous plughole.

"Stand back!" Mr Morley, who has the habit of appearing whenever there's trouble, pushes his way through and crouches over the prostrate teacher. "Margaret, this is Ken," he booms, as if Miss Wilson has fallen down a mineshaft or something. "Do you need a doctor? Where does it hurt?"

"Euurrrraaaggggh," goes Miss Wilson, her eyes fluttering dramatically.

"I think she might be a bit winded, sir," I suggest.

10

"Well spotted," goes Lisa under her breath.

"I knew you girls needed supervision," says Mr Morley, helping Miss Wilson into a sitting position.

"What?" says Lisa. "If it wasn't for Miss Wilson getting in the way of – "

"Don't speak ill of the winded," mutters Ellie.

By now Miss Wilson has managed to heave herself to her feet and, supported with some difficulty by Mr Morley, she starts to make her way, with the occasional tragic moan, back to the school building.

"I'm going to have to look at the whole question of the Metropolitan Cup," says Mr Morley over his shoulder. "It can be a dangerous game, football. Maybe it's not suitable for – " He chokes back the sexist statement he's about to make at the last minute. "Not suitable for . . . the playground."

"It's not football that's dangerous," says Tara. "It's Roberta's left foot."

"Yeah, you need a licence for that thing," says Lisa. "It's a lethal weapon."

"All right!" Tears have filled Roberta's eyes. "I feel bad about it already."

"Told you football and girls didn't go together."

We look up to see Jason, Dominic and Robert walking towards us, hands in pockets.

"It's a man's game, ennit." Jason smirks as he picks up our ball and begins to juggle it on his right foot in the way I've never been able to manage.

"Shut up it's a man's game," says Tara.

"You'd look like Miss Wilson if you'd had one of Roberta's left footers in your back," says Ellie.

11

"That little tap? That ... powderpuff? You're joking." Jason throws the ball to Dominic.

"You should stick to netball, girls," says Dominic, gaining courage from the great god Jason.

The rest of the girls who had made up the teams are drifting out of the playground now, leaving the hard-core Hotshots standing by the goal.

"Tell you what," Tara says suddenly, "I feel like a bit of goalkeeping practice. Why don't we have a penalty shoot-out? You three take shots at me in goal and we'll have a go against you."

The boys collapse in spasms of incredulous mockery.

"Forget it, Tara," says Jason. "We'd blast you through the back of the net. They'd have to lay you out beside old Wilson."

Without a word, Tara turns towards the goal, pulling on her yellow goalkeeping gloves. "Try it," she goes.

It takes about a minute for the boys, with a lot of pushing and jeering and lamebrain discussion, to work out which one of them is going to take the first kick. Eventually, Robert grabs the ball and puts it on the penalty spot.

You don't have to be brilliant to see that scoring a penalty in the playground is not exactly difficult. The spot's marked close to the goal and, unless the goal-keeper actually enjoys throwing herself to the ground on concrete, all you have to do is aim for the corner of the net.

This Robert does, to whoops of delight from the other boys.

It's our turn to take a shot. After Jason has swaggered

into goal, stupid grin all over his face, Lisa puts the ball down, runs up – and blasts the ball about a yard over the top of the goal.

More oafish cheers from the male team. "One nil, one nil, one nil," they chant.

Grimly, Tara steps back into goal. Dominic picks up the ball and places it on the spot.

Have you heard about players blessed with a "football brain"? Dominic has one of those – he's got the brain of a football. After a short run-up, he aims the ball for precisely the same spot as Robert did.

Only this time Tara – the bravest goalkeeper in the world – is ready for it. Diving to her right, her body scraping along the concrete, she deflects the ball around the far right post. For a moment she lays in a crumpled heap on the ground before painfully getting to her feet. She dusts herself down, glances up at Dominic, who still can't believe that she has saved it, and winks. That girl has style.

Jason's back in goal now. He makes a typically racist remark as Charlie places the ball on the penalty spot. She doesn't bother to respond but contemptuously hits the ball past him to make it 1–1 with one more shot each to go.

By now, a small crowd of first-year children has gathered beyond the wire fence to watch.

"Right, little girl." Jason isn't smiling any more as he stands over the ball staring at Tara in goal. "Prepare to meet thy doom."

It's totally obvious what Jason is going to do – use his strength to blast the ball straight at Tara. Not only

13

will it knock her backwards into the net (he thinks), but, with a bit of luck, it will do her a bit of damage too. Jason's a great believer in brute force and ignorance.

He takes a three-pace run and fires a shot with all the force in his right foot.

But Tara stands, solid and strong. As Jason's rocket hits her outstretched hands, the crack echoes around the playground. The ball bounces high and wide over the top of the goal.

There's a moment of astonished silence. Then Tara walks out of the goalmouth. Only as she turns away, the palms of her hands tucked into her armpits, can we see the tears of pain in her eyes.

Our last shot. If we can score, we've won. But who's going to take that last penalty? Tara is in no fit state to kick the ball. Ellie bruised her ankle during the game and can't kick the ball with any power. As we turn to Roberta, she shakes her head firmly.

"I don't want to," she says quietly. "Not after what happened to Miss Wilson."

'It's got to be you," goes Lisa. "Tara can hardly walk, Ellie's injured and Eve – " her glance in my direction says it all.

"For the Hotshots, Roberta," I say.

Jason is swaying cockily in goal as Roberta carefully places the ball on the penalty spot. She steps back, looks down to compose herself, like a pianist before a concert, takes one pace forward – and lets her left foot do the rest.

I swear I've never seen her hit the ball harder. It

screams through the air catching Jason full in the stomach. He crumples backwards into the net, and the ball follows him.

2–1.

We slap Roberta on the back and hurry over to where Jason is painfully untangling himself from the net.

"Sorry, Jason." Roberta looks like she's going to cry again. "Are you all right? I didn't mean to hurt you."

"Hurt? That powd—" Jason's voice comes out like an asthmatic wheeze.

"Shut up, powderpuff," says Tara. "You can hardly breathe."

"Be – beginner's luck." Jason makes his way slowly back to where Dominic and Robert are standing in silence, aghast that their idol has been humiliated. He glances back at us before the three of them walk towards the school gate, muttering dark plans of revenge.

I watch them for a moment. Jason is no actor and what he's feeling towards the Hotshots right now is as clear as the pain on his face.

It's respect.

Talking of respect, the time has come to take you to a place where Respect for Others is one of the basic house rules.

It's seven-thirty that night. I have just finished my homework and I'm helping my mother cook the supper which, because it's Tuesday, will be pasta followed by fruit salad. Soon my father will wander into the kitchen, having left his copy of the *Guardian* carefully folded in the sitting-room and say, "Hmmm, smells good. What's on the menu tonight, Jennifer?" My mother will mutter something affectionate as he peers over her shoulder.

Get the picture?

In my total innocence, I'm telling Mum about the decline and fall of Miss Wilson that afternoon in the playground.

"Euuurrrrghh." I stagger around the kitchen in a rather brilliant imitation. "And, her face is all dark, eyes popping out of her head. For a moment, we were really scared. *Euuuurrraaaaggghhh!*"

"Eve!" My mother frowns as she stirs something on the cooker. "Please stop making that noise. It's so . . . unfeminine."

"And Mr Morley's leaning over her, going, 'Can you hear me, Elizabeth?'" I laugh at the memory.

"It all sounds very rough and nasty," says my mother, smiling. "I'm not sure I approve of teachers being brutalized in the playground." She dips a little finger into the sauce she's making and tastes it. "Roberta could get sued for assault."

"Assault! It was Miss Wilson's fault for not ducking."

"Hmmm, smells good. What's on the menu tonight, Jennifer?"

My father, wearing a brown corduroy suit and a washed-out look, makes his entry.

"Fettucine," says my mother. "Eve's team has claimed its first victim. A teacher was knocked over in the playground."

"Ah." My father slumps down at the kitchen table,

16

as if this news was the latest of many terrible things that have happened to him that day. "The dreaded soccer team."

"Suppertime," says my mother quickly, in a doomed attempt to head off a lecture from my father about what girls should do and what girls shouldn't do.

A look of intense irritation has settled on my father's face. He hates football. In his mind, he associates the game with a load of crop-headed boys jumping all over one another whenever they score a goal. The idea of his "little one", as he likes to call me, becoming a football player has already been cue for total trauma. When I first told him about the Hotshots and the Metropolitan Cup, he expressed what he called "the most serious reservations".

"As you know, Eve," he goes, "I yield to no one in my belief in an all-round education – " (this is how my father talks, by the way – even when he loses his temper, he speaks as if he's reading from a speech written by someone else) " – but I find myself questioning whether it's entirely appropriate for you to be playing soccer at this time. New school, exams soon – why are you rolling your eyes, Eve?"

"Nothing," I sigh.

"What about your recorder lessons?" he continues.

"And ballet," my mother chimes in.

Great. I'm getting it in stereo now.

"It's my way of relaxing," I say quietly. Suddenly I don't feel hungry any more.

"But you love the recorder and ballet," says my mother.

17

"I do?" I look her straight in the eye. "Thanks for telling me, Mum."

"That's quite enough of your rudeness, Eve Simpson." My father slaps the table. "I don't like this aggressive tone of voice which I've been hearing recently. I find myself wondering where you've learnt it. On the football pitch perhaps." Pleased with this brilliant deduction, he sits back in his chair. "I propose that you tell the Hotshots to make their way in the Cup without you."

"What?" I can't believe my ears.

"Are you one of their key players?" My father gives me a wintry little smile. "With those skinny little legs of yours?"

I stand up. "I like football," I say through gritted teeth. "I may not be the best player in the world but I like it."

Before my father can get into another speech, I walk out of the kitchen, past his neat little office, up the perfectly brushed stairs and into my room where I sweep the carefully arranged pencils on to the floor. Crying, I sit on the edge of the bed and flick a finger at the door, just like Tara has that afternoon.

Only, with me, it just feels stupid.

I walk to the upstairs telephone and dial Tara's number. As usual, it sounds as if World War III is breaking out at the Williams house as her mother picks up the phone – a baby crying, TV blaring, the booming tones of Mr Williams in the background. With some difficulty, I manage to get Mrs Williams to understand that I need to talk to Tara.

"Hi, Hotshot." When Tara comes on the line, she's

clearly still flying high after this afternoon's penalty shoot-out. For a few minutes, she yaks on about the game, Miss Wilson, who would coach us now, the look on Jason's face as he untangled himself from the net . . .

Tara has never exactly been little Miss Sensitive but eventually it occurs to her that I haven't said anything.

"Something wrong?" she asks. "Why did you call?"

"I think I'm leaving the Hotshots," I say gloomily.

"Shut up you're leaving the Hotshots."

"It's my parents."

"Eh?" Tara has never understood my home life. "What's their problem exactly?"

"Fun. It's against their religion."

"Oh, lame," goes Tara. "If you don't play, we might as well pack up the Hotshots."

"You mean – ?"

But before I can express my surprise, she adds, "It's not that you're good at football or anything, just, if you're not around to arrange things, nothing will get done, will it?"

"Thanks, Tara. You've made me feel a whole lot better."

My mother's calling me back to the kitchen.

"Gotta go," I say. "I'm on parade again."

I put the phone down and stand there, thinking.

On their first day of official practice for the Met Cup, the Hotshots have injured their coach, annoyed the headteacher, turned the school bully into a mortal enemy, my parents have banned me from playing and now Tara's talking about scrapping the whole thing.

Great start.

CHAPTER TWO

Dead Meat

Suddenly no one wants to talk about the Hotshots any more.

Ever since the felling of Miss Wilson, there's been a rumour going around that Morley is going to ban us from playing. Now and then a few of us kick a ball around after school but, for the moment at least, our heart isn't in it.

Then, on Friday afternoon, the headteacher calls us to his study to hear his verdict.

"As you all know, Miss Wilson has recovered after the accident but she still feels rather . . . fragile and won't be able to take your practice game next Tuesday," he says sitting behind his desk with an apologetic smile which I just know means bad news is on the way. "It appears that no other member of staff has the time resources to take her place. So – " Mr Morley shrugs helplessly.

"We'll take ourselves," says Lisa quickly. "You remember what you said. Don't follow leaders – "

"You need supervision. While in the school grounds, you're my responsibility. If there were another accident we'd all be in trouble."

"What about a parent, sir?" I ask, but as the words leave my lips, I know it's a hopeless idea. The Hotshots' parents are almost as disorganized as their children.

"Possible, I suppose." The headteacher glances at his watch. "But I'd need to have a volunteer parent by Monday. Otherwise I'll be withdrawing the team from the Cup. All right?" He reaches for some papers on his desk and we shuffle disconsolately out of the room.

"Why does this never happen to the boys?" mutters Roberta in the corridor outside his office.

"Because teachers like taking them," says Lisa. "If Jason had flattened Miss Wilson with a ball, they'd all be saying, 'Great kick on him, that boy.'"

"Maybe we can ask my dad to be manager." This is Tara's brilliant idea. "He likes football."

Each of us tries to imagine Mr Williams, a man not exactly blessed with the patience of a saint, prancing about the playground with us.

"Yeah, maybe not," goes Tara, reading our thoughts.

"Mr Phelan," I say suddenly.

They look at me as if I'm crazy.

"Who's Mr Phelan?" asks Ellie.

"Patrick's dad. I remember hearing that he managed the boys' team when Patrick was in his first year."

Even if memories of his father are hazy, everyone knows Patrick. He's three years ahead of us, but he's already making a name for himself as a school hero. Good looking, a great athlete, charming, top in every lesson, Patrick is the Boy with Everything.

"Why on earth would this Mr Phelan want to help?" Roberta asks.

"He likes football," I shrug. "It's worth a go."

"He won't be interested in managing a girls' team, no way," goes Tara.

"Maybe . . . Maybe it *is* worth a go." A distant look has appeared in Lisa's eyes. "They live in the block of flats near where I live."

Now here's a surprise. Lisa's not exactly the type to volunteer normally – the phrase "Look after Number One" might have been invented for her.

"Yeah, in fact, it's a great idea, Eve," she's saying. "I'll call round there tonight."

Charlie's smiling. "Just because you fancy Patrick," she says.

We all look at Lisa, who has the grace to blush. "If anything, he fancies me. He's always following me around in break."

"How could you?" goes Roberta. "He's such a poser with that hair flopping over his eyes."

"I think he's quite nice actually," mutters Ellie.

"We're here to talk about football not about who fancies Patrick Phelan," booms Tara. "I vote Eve goes round with Lisa. Just to make sure she remembers what to say."

Before Lisa can take offence, I jump in. "Two heads are better than one, eh, Lis?"

With an angry flash of her green eyes, Lisa nods her agreement.

*

There are some parts of this city where, even on a hot June evening, the sun doesn't seem to reach. The Prospect Estate is one of those places. It's only a five-minute walk from the road where Lisa and I live yet, with its grey, towering buildings and crumbling walls covered with graffiti, it might belong to a different universe.

"I'm not sure this was such a good idea," Lisa mutters as we push our way through the heavy door of the tower block where the Phelans live. "This place looks like Muggers' Row."

Ignoring her, I press the button for the lift. The door opens slowly and, trying to ignore the smell of disinfectant, we step in. By now, a look of distaste has settled on Lisa's pale features.

On the tenth floor, we walk along a stone corridor and knock on the Phelans' door.

No reply.

"Not to worry." Lisa turns to go.

As I knock again, there are sounds of movement from inside, followed by a wheezy cough.

"Who is it?" The reedy, broken voice seems too old, more that of a grandfather than a father.

"Eve and Lisa," I shout. "We're friends of Patrick's."

"He's out in the park or somewhere . . ." The voice trails off wearily.

"It was you we wanted to talk to, Mr Phelan," I call out.

There's the sound of a bolt being drawn back. The door opens slightly to reveal Mr Phelan, unshaven, his eyes bloodshot, his complexion puffy and unhealthy.

23

"What would you be wanting me for, then?" he asks, his eyes half closing as the smoke from a cigarette stuck in the side of his mouth plumes upwards.

"Maybe . . . nothing," Lisa says, half to herself.

"It's about a football team." I step forward. "A girls' football team."

Gerry Phelan coughs again, sending ash down his grubby white shirt. "Football?" He sighs as if people were always coming to the front door to bother him with talk of football teams. "Well, you'd better come in, I suppose."

As he opens the door, a stale pub-like smell wafts unpleasantly from the dark hall behind him. "Sorry about the – " He gestures vaguely at the mayhem around him: empty beer bottles, old newspapers, full ashtrays, dust, a couple of coffee cups gathering mould.

"Would you say that this place lacks a woman's touch?" Lisa murmurs out of the side of her mouth as we follow Mr Phelan in to a small, dusty sitting-room where a TV flickers soundlessly in the corner.

I smile. Patrick's mother, I remember now, walked out some five years ago.

Mr Phelan lowers himself into an armchair. One of his toes, I can't help noticing, is peeking through a hole in the battered old bedroom slippers he's wearing. "So tell me about this football team."

Lisa does the talking. (For some reason, Lisa always does the talking – either she's a natural leader or one of life's egomaniacs.)

As she talks, I think back to the last time I saw

24

Patrick's father. It was in the playground and the school team was playing St Cuthbert's, our local rivals. Patrick scored a hat trick, as usual. Striding up and down the touchline, Gerry Phelan was a different man that day from this sad, half-drunken wreck.

He smiles as Lisa reaches the end of her account.

"So, no one will manage you?" He lights another cigarette and inhales deeply. "What's wrong with your teachers?"

"It's extra work." I manage to get a word in edgeways at last. "I think they just want to go home at the end of the day."

"Of course you might be too busy," says Lisa, her voice a bit too eager to be polite.

"Busy?" Mr Phelan laughs bitterly. "Hardly." After a moment's silence, he asks, "Got a goalkeeper?"

"The best," I say.

"Striker?"

"That's me," says Lisa. "I score a lot of goals."

"Good." Mr Phelan rubs his eyes as if he's just waking up. "I'll give you a trial."

Lisa winces noticeably. "I'm not sure – "

"Thanks, Mr Phelan," I interrupt. At this stage, I'm not exactly keen on the idea of Mr Phelan, in his stained collarless shirt and old bedroom slippers, becoming the Hotshots manager, but it's too late to change our minds.

"Tuesday?" he asks.

"Four o'clock," I smile.

"See you then." Mr Phelan nods briskly. "Let yourselves out, girls."

"Phew," I say, as we emerge gulping at the fresh air outside. "Poor Patrick, having to live with that."

"We didn't even *see* Patrick." Lisa is pouting angrily as she strides across the wasteland on which a group of small, smut-faced boys are chasing a skinny dog. "And now we've got a drunken old shufflebum as manager thanks to your brilliant idea."

"Excuse me," I say. "We weren't there to see your darling Patrick. Anyway I wasn't to know Mr Phelan was a drunk."

"What are we going to do now?"

"Maybe he won't turn up."

"Hope not," grumbles Lisa. "Some of us have a reputation to think of."

Lisa and her reputation. That's a laugh.

When we return that evening, she casually suggests that I call by after supper so that we can work together on our maths homework.

"Work together" in Lisa-speak involves her toying with her hair and talking about herself while I do her sums for her.

So why do I agree? Because there's something about Lisa's shameless vanity that I can't help liking. Because I love to slop about her house, drinking Coke, eating chocolates and talking about boys as if we were nineteen or something. And maybe because, in my innocent little heart, I believe that just a tiny part of Lisa's glamour, her confidence in everything she does, will rub off on me.

26

"Evie! Honey! Hi!"

Oddly enough, Lisa's mother Mrs Martin (Yasmin, would you believe?) is at home when I call round. A tall woman with unnaturally blonde hair, she greets me at the door with a shriek of joy and a kiss on each cheek. She's wearing a skimpy T-shirt which shows her belly button and jeans so tight they look as if they've been sprayed on. Mrs Martin is an actress.

"Hi," I say uncertainly. "Is Lisa at home please, Mrs Martin?"

"Mrs Martin, Mrs Martin." She mimics me as she waves me in, spilling some of the drink that's in her right hand. "I've told you, Evie love, I'm Yasmin. Mrs Martin makes me sound so *old*."

"Sorry . . . Yasmin."

The design and size of Lisa's house is the same as mine. Everything else is different. There are clothes and magazines and photographs and videos strewn everywhere. At home, you have to be careful where you sit, you worry if you're bringing dirt into the house; here you can totally relax. I follow Mrs Martin into the dark sitting-room where Lisa's lolling on the floor in front of the television.

"Hi," she says, with no more than the briefest of glances in my direction.

Mrs Martin lights up a cigarette and begins pacing back and forth. "Maybe Evie will help me with my lines," she says sulkily. "Since my own flesh and blood won't help me."

"It's only an ad, Mum." Lisa stares at the TV screen.

"You'll probably only have to say, 'I don't believe it, they're so white!'"

"God, you can be such a bitch sometimes, Lisa," says Mrs Martin. "You have no idea of the pressure in this business."

Whistling quietly to herself, Lisa switches off the TV. "Shall we go upstairs?" she says to me. "We can get a bit of peace up there."

"I'm quite happy to help with the lines if – "

"No, no." Mrs Martin dismisses us with a tragic wave of the hand. "You go and talk about your football. I'm sure that's *much* more interesting."

"Sorry about that," Lisa says as we walk up the stairs. "She's just been dumped by her new boyfriend."

Now this is what I like most about visiting Lisa's house. There's always some great drama unfolding. It's as good as any soap opera.

"I've got used to the routine now," Lisa's saying. "Love. Pain. Despair. Vodka. Then love again. We're on the vodka stage right now."

A telephone rang in the hall downstairs.

"It's for you-ou," Mrs Martin called out. "Someone called Dominic."

"Dominic?" Lisa frowns. "What on earth can he want?"

"Don't be long," Mrs Martin says more quietly. "I have an urgent call to make."

In spite of almost falling over the banisters in my attempts to eavesdrop, I hear little of the conversation. "No," Lisa seems to be saying. "Not now . . . bad moment . . . ring back, yeah."

"Not Dominic from school?" I ask when she returns.

"Nah. Dominic, my cousin." She gives an unconvincing little smile.

I'm just thinking that, if Lisa really wants to be an actress, she has a long way to go, when she says rather crossly, "Are we going to do some work or just chat?"

Sighing, I follow her into her room. She clears the magazines from her desk for me, then stretches out on the bed.

From downstairs can be heard the brittle tones of Mrs Martin as she makes her urgent call. "Gavin, darling, it's Yasmin. We met at Mel's party last week. You remember, I'm the Virgo – " a peel of girlish giggles filled the house.

"Sounds like she's on to the next stage in the routine," I say quietly.

Lisa's examining the ends of her heavy dark hair. "Please don't laugh at my mother," she says coolly.

As soon as Gerry Phelan arrives at Broadhurst Comprehensive the following Tuesday afternoon, it's clear that he has made a real effort to look like a human being. The bedroom slippers have gone, to be replaced by a pair of battered old trainers. Instead of jeans, he wears a tracksuit. And as he makes his way through a group of disapproving parents into the school playground and stands on the touchline, he doesn't seem to be drunk.

"Uh-oh," Lisa mutters under her breath, as we take practice shots at goal. "Looks like he didn't forget, after all."

"Go and say hello to him, then." Roberta is trying not to stare. "You invited him."

"I thought he'd bring Patrick," says Lisa feebly.

"Honestly, you and Patrick." Roberta chips the ball towards the goal.

"What about me and Patrick?"

Leaving them to bicker, I walk over to our new trainer.

"Welcome to the Hotshots, Mr Phelan," I say nervously.

"Good to see you, Eve." His hooded eyes glance at me, then back at the players in front of goal. "So when's training meant to begin?"

"Any time, Mr Phelan."

He reaches into his pocket and pulls out a silver whistle. The piercing blast turns heads in the playground. The Hotshots gather up the ball and run to where he stands, pushing and laughing and chatting.

"I'm Gerry Phelan," he says, when some sort of calm has descended on the group. "I've been told you have a football team here." Despite his appearance, there's a quiet authority in Mr Phelan's voice. "I've been watching you practise and I have to say that, if that's your idea of football, you'll be winning absolutely nothing."

"Eh? We're good." Tara, of course, is the first to object.

Mr Phelan fixes her with those piercing grey eyes of his. To my utter astonishment, Tara actually looks embarrassed.

"Give us that ball," he says.

Roberta throws Mr Phelan the ball, which he bounces on the ground, then flicks up with his left foot.

"Where are the other balls?" he asks.

"We're only allowed one," says Ellie. "The boys use five but Mr Morley says we'll lose them."

Mr Phelan frowns. "We need five. And training shirts."

"I think you'll have to ask Mr Morley for those," says Lisa.

"Morley? Oh, the head man, right."

Something's niggling at the back of my mind. "You have spoken to the headteacher about this, haven't you?" I ask. "I mean, he does know you're the new coach?"

"All in due time," says Mr Phelan easily. "Now let's see how fit you are."

Our new manager, despite looking about as healthy as something out of *The Night of the Living Dead*, turns out to be a great believer in fitness.

You thought that playing football was a question of kicking a ball about, with the general idea of getting it into the other team's net, right?

Wrong. According to our new manager, the most important part of training is done without the ball.

So we run.

We jump.

We stretch.

We run some more.

There are dark mutterings from some of the girls – I mean, this isn't even *fun* – but something about Mr

Phelan as he stands there, giving instructions in that quiet voice, keeps us going.

After about twenty minutes' agony, he gathers us around him once more.

"Now that we've got you . . . warmed up," he smiles palely, "we're going to have a practice match."

"I say." The unmistakable voice of Mr Morley makes all of us turn – all of us, that is, except Mr Phelan.

"Right," he's going. "Let's divide you into teams. Which is your first team defence?"

"Excuse me." The head is now standing two yards away from us.

"Sir?" Gerry Phelan turns slowly. "How can I help you?"

"You can help me by explaining what you're doing with these girls."

"Training them." Mr Phelan smiles politely. "They're going to win the Metropolitan Cup."

"I'm not aware that you're a member of staff," says Mr Morley.

"I'm a parent, sir. Patrick Phelan's my boy."

"I don't see Patrick in the playground. So perhaps you could oblige me by leaving the school premises."

A deep colour suffuses Mr Phelan's cheeks and, for a moment, he seems lost for words. It's at this moment that I realize that, while he might be a good trainer, the man has no idea how to deal with someone in authority, like Mr Morley.

Lisa nudges me. "Say something," she murmurs.

"It's my fault, sir," I blurt out.

Dead Meat

The headteacher's eyes turn slowly towards me. "Your fault, Eve?" he asks dangerously.

"Yes, sir," I say, the professional fall girl as usual. "You said you wanted a parent to supervise us. None of our mums or dads had the time, so I asked Mr Phelan here. And he agreed."

"But I meant one of your parents. Surely even you lot could understand that."

"I've been a Broadhurst manager before," says Mr Phelan suddenly. "When I coached the first year we beat all the local schools. We were the best team in the area."

Mr Morley's eyes narrow. A track record of success is never going to win him round.

"How very impressive," he says acidly. "You have twenty minutes to finish your practice, Mr Phelan," he adds, glancing at his watch. "After that, the Hotshots will be disbanded. I will not countenance having unauthorized personnel in the school grounds."

"Suit yourself." Mr Phelan turns his back on the headteacher. "Right, girls – " He smiles as if nothing has happened. "Play your game as usual – I need to see what you're all made of."

As we take up our positions on the pitch, the Head says something else to Mr Phelan, who shrugs wordlessly.

Maybe it's the tension, or the fact that, from all round the playground, we're being watched by parents, teachers and other children. Just possibly, Gerry Phelan has managed to inspire us in some quiet, mysterious way. Whatever the reason, we play brilliantly that afternoon.

Lisa dances around the pitch, the ball apparently attached to her right foot by an invisible magnet. Charlie is rock-like in defence. For a change, Roberta and Ellie are giving the game 100 per cent concentration as they pass the ball around with casual ease. Tara throws herself about heroically in goal.

The twenty minutes pass quickly and, as we troop off the pitch after a 3–3 draw, Mr Phelan calls us round.

"I have one word for what I've seen this afternoon," he says quietly, "and that's . . . adequate. So, before we go any further with this mallarkey, you have to answer me this question. Are we here for fun – or to play winning football?"

"Play winning football," we all mutter dutifully.

"Right. I'm glad you said that because, if you hadn't, I'd have been off to see that headteacher of yours and I'd have said, 'Take 'em, my friend – Gerry Phelan wants nothing to do with them.' So, if you want to play winning football, here's your first lesson. I'll tell you this once and once only. You're here to compete, not chat. You two – " he points to Tara and Charlie – "were chatting away like a couple of washerwomen."

"Eh?" A moody pout appears on Tara's face.

"There's one subject of conversation on that pitch and that's the game. Call for the ball. Help your team members. Make them aware of where you are."

He looks hard at Lisa.

"You're not bad as a player," he says, "but you're one

of the worst team members I've ever seen. I'll be having no prima donnas in this outfit. It doesn't matter who scores the goal as long as it's for your team, not against it."

Lisa looks away moodily.

"Now another thing – you've got to forget your nice upbringing. If someone falls over, you don't stop to see whether she's all right. Listen for the whistle. If the ref hasn't blown, you keep playing. And you don't – " he glares at me – "run up to the referee and admit you touched the ball."

"Just being sportsmanlike," I mutter.

"Forget your perfect manners. The sides you'll be up against in the Met will be tough, hard."

Lisa puts up her hand.

"But we're not in the Met," she says. "The head-teacher said – "

"Never mind that. Anyone who wants me to coach them will be in the park after school tomorrow." He gives a rare smile. "Tell your parents Gerry Phelan's in charge."

As Mr Phelan walks out of the playground, I wink at Tara. The world may be against us but at least we have a coach who seems to have faith in us.

"I don't like him," mutters Lisa. "Anyway, I do pass the ball."

"No way was I chatting," says Tara.

"He's taking us seriously." Roberta's smiling to herself. "He's treating us as if we really wanted to win rather than a load of girls doing something that's a bit of a laugh."

"Yeah, well, there's no need for him to be rude," says Lisa.

"He had only seen us for a few minutes but he could immediately see what was wrong with us." This is Ellie. "And he's right. We're playing as if it were the Lisa and Tara Show. We need to think as a team."

"Why does he want us to meet him in the park?" asks Charlie.

"Because we're just Hotshots now," I say quietly. "You don't have to be entered in the Cup by your school – so Mr Morley can't stop us."

"Yes." Tara punches the air. "We're not a school team any more. We're free – just so long as our parents give permission."

I sigh. Trust Tara to bring me down.

A confession: after the argument over football, I've decided that, until my parents get used to the basic concept of Hotshots, I'll have to tell a few lies when it comes to explaining where I'm spending my time. They don't exactly know I'm still playing football.

This afternoon, for example, I'm meant to be at Tara's house, helping her with a geography project.

It's only a temporary lie, I've told myself.

And I'm right.

When I get in that evening, my mother and father are already there, having tea in the sitting-room – they both work in the offices of the local council and, on the days when my mother's working full-time, they travel home together, chatting and smiling and telling one another about the fascinating day they've had at work. Lisa once said I was lucky to have parents like this – hers takes out new boyfriends like other people take out videos – but I'm not so sure.

Sometimes – like this afternoon – I feel almost like an intruder. As I walk in, I can almost see their happy-couple smiles fading away to be replaced by the furrowed brows of careworn parents.

"Hi," I go, standing in the doorway.

"Hello, Eve," says my mother. "We were worried about you. You're late."

"I told you. I had to see Tara about her homework. Honestly, she's got no clue, that girl. She doesn't even know what urbanization is, let alone how to write about it. I thought I was bad at geography but she . . ."

You know how it is when you're lying – you just have to say too much, don't you? By the time I've finished, I've told them more than I thought I knew about land masses, how Tara's brothers and sisters had kept interrupting, how we had been delayed by her mother offering us tea, what her mother had been wearing . . .

For a moment, an accusing silence fills the sitting-room.

"Why are you blushing, Eve?" my mother asks eventually.

"Blushing?" I touch my forehead. "I'm just a bit hot."

Ah! Fool! There's another silence as my father lets this gaffe hang in the air before delivering his killer blow.

"Hot work, was it, this geography?" he asks with a hint of sarcasm in his voice.

"You've hurt your leg," says my mother.

I look down. There's a scrape on my knee from where I have fallen over in the park while almost scoring a goal.

It's official. I am now dead meat.

Unlike a really expert liar – Tara, for instance – it takes just one little puff to blow away my carefully constructed alibis.

"I nearly scored a goal," I say sulkily.

There's another silence, during which my father stares miserably into space. It's as if I've just told him that I'm a crazed glue-sniffing drug addict or something. "Go to your room," he says quietly.

Suddenly I find strength from somewhere. I think of all the work I've put into the Hotshots. I think of how I persuaded Mr Phelan to supervise us. I think of how he'd stood up to the headteacher.

"You always said that it was important to be enthusiastic," I say. "Well, I am – about football. Just because it's not something you approve of, like ballet or music, you want to stop me doing it. Well, I don't care. I'm going to do it. I played well today. Our new coach Mr Phelan said I was really good." This last lie I managed with total sincerity.

You know the saying, divide and rule? It's right. Only, with parents, it's more like divide and survive. My father will never like football but Mum's different – she knows what it's like to be a girl growing up in a world where men are still making most of the rules. So, when my eyes filled with tears, I turn them on her.

"It's my life," I say.

My mother looks across the table to my father. "Maybe we should talk about this, Matthew," she says to my father.

I think I just scored a goal.

CHAPTER THREE

*No one likes us,
we don't care*

Tanned, rich, athletic, American – yes, almost everything about Stevie Rostand made me suspicious at first. In those days when she used to laugh at what we were doing in the Hotshots, I remember listing in my head my reasons for disliking her.

1. She has a sort of glowing good health that's almost an insult to the rest of us. Look at her skin, her muscle tone, and you would think that she had been brought up on better food, breathing better air than the rest of us. Yet she's lived in the same grimy London environment as us for the past two years, and likes the same junk food.

2. When she goes on holiday, she doesn't just go to Scotland or Cornwall – it's the West Indies or Florida. As a result she has the same tan all year round. Almost as annoying is her long dark hair

which she lets fall over her eyes in an affected sort of way.

3. She wears about £300-worth of designer clothes to school.

4. Because she's always going back to the States, she knows about films way before we do. Worse, she's always coming into school with some new computer game which the rest of us have never heard of.

5. Which is why the boys love her. The rest of us could just about stand her – she can be really funny sometimes – if it weren't for the fact that she hangs out with Jason and his Neanderthal crew. This, I'm afraid, puts her beyond the pale. There's a limit to our tolerance.

As part of her campaign to be Little Miss Different, Stevie Rostand ignores the Hotshots but joins in the general excitement when, the evening before our first game, the boys are victorious in their first round of the Met Cup.

"They were just so cool, you wouldn't believe it," she drawls the following morning as we're waiting for the first lesson to begin. "Different class to the other teams, you know."

"Did you see that little dummy I did, Stevie?" Jason calls out. "Sent their defender the wrong way, then – blam! Goodnight nurse."

"Yeah, you'd be good at dummies," Lisa says loudly. "Being one yourself."

"Yaaaaahhhh." Jason gives one of his typically intelligent replies, with appropriate gestures.

"And tonight it's sayonara Hotshots," says Stevie.

See what I mean? She has to say it. And Tara – who else? – has to react.

She strides up to Stevie's desk. "Shut up sayonara Hotshots," she says, as if she knows what Stevie's talking about. "Yank." She pushes a pile of Stevie's books on to the floor.

"What's your damage, you dork!" Stevie leaps to her feet. Luckily it's at that moment that Mr Thomas, our maths teacher, shambles in, to head off what might have become a major international incident.

But Stevie Rostand's mockery doesn't worry us any more than the fact that, ever since Mr Morley's argument with Gerry Phelan, there's been a general "do not mention the Hotshots" rule among the teachers, although we've been practising every Tuesday and Thursday after school. The head can't actually stop us taking part but, because we're no longer the school team, we won't enjoy any of the advantages the boys had.

There will be no school van to take us tonight, so we'll take the bus. We're not allowed to use the school kit – Mr Phelan has had to borrow some horrible old purple shirts from a local boys' team.

It's weird how this has affected us all. We're simply more determined than ever. During Mr Thomas's lesson, I catch Roberta's eye and we smile at one another. Tara, I notice, is writhing around in her seat

42

as if, in the middle of maths, she's keeping goal. At one point, Lisa's practising her I've-scored-a-goal gesture – the second finger of each hand pointing to the sky – when Mr Thomas thinks that she's trying to ask a question. It's that sort of day.

After school, our friends quietly wish us luck as the six of us – Tara, Lisa, Ellie, Roberta, Charlie and me – leave for the bus stop. There's almost a sense of conspiracy now, as if we're a sort of secret army, going off to fight in a war no one will admit is going on.

It's Tara who first starts us singing as we walk down the High Street. "We are Hotshots, we are Hotshots. No one likes us, we don't care – "

"What on earth's that?" laughs Lisa.

"I heard it at a football match," says Tara, swinging her kit bag as she walks. "It's what the fans of really unpopular teams sing – like, their anthem."

Soon we're all at it, yelling at the top of our voices all about how we're Hotshots, how no one likes us and how we don't care.

As we make our way down the High Street, shoppers part before us, some of them tutting away at our behaviour.

I smile as I sing. So what if it isn't ladylike? Who cares if girls aren't exactly supposed to walk down the street in a bunch, singing their lungs out?

We are Hotshots, we don't care.

There's a shock in store for us when we reach the bus stop. Our manager is there but at first we don't recognize him. He's actually wearing a dark suit and shiny black shoes. He looks like someone coming home after a hard day at the office.

"What happened, Mr Phelan?" asks Tara with her usual tact. "Has someone in the family died?"

Mr Phelan gives a little smile. "Big day," he says simply.

On the bus, even Tara has gone quiet. I find myself wondering what I'm doing in this team and thinking back to our last practice in the park . . .

Mr Phelan stands on the touchline, shouting advice. As play continues, he takes each of the Hotshot players aside and talks to them about their game.

When it comes to my turn, he looks at me with that smile of his. "I've told Lisa about lay-offs and tap-ins," he says. "I've explained to the wide players the need for a perfect square ball every time – "

Lay-off? I'm thinking to myself. Perfect square ball? What's he talking about?

"Then with Charlie I've looked at the block tackle, how your defence has to stand up to the opposing striker." He hesitates. "And now I'm trying to think what I can tell you. What position d'you like playing in best, Eve?"

"I'm substitute," I said. "I go wherever I'm told."

"But where do you feel most at home?"

On the touchline, I want to tell him. In front of a television. Anywhere but on that pitch. I wish this was cricket, so that I could be the scorer.

"I just run and kick the ball," I say eventually.

He winks and pats me on the back. "Go back on and play your normal game," he says.

"All right, Eve?" Mr Phelan's smiling at me across the gangway of the bus. Although it's only three weeks since Lisa and I visited him at his flat, something about him has changed. He's sober now, of course, and he has taken off his bedroom slippers, but there's an alertness to him. I just hope that the Hotshots don't let him down.

It's a short walk through grimy streets from the bus stop to the youth club where the first round of the Met Cup is to take place.

As we approach the large Victorian building, an anxious silence descends on our group. Already players from other schools and teams are gathering outside the door. Everyone except us seems to have brought a few carloads of supporters with them.

"What's with the Old Bill?" asks Tara as we enter the club. "There are policemen everywhere."

"Say it a bit louder, why don't you?" says Roberta. "Then we'll get arrested before we've played a game."

"The police run the competition," I explain. "That's why it's called the Metropolitan Cup. Metropolitan Police, see? It helps their image in the community."

"Right, that's it, I'm off," says Tara. "I'm not helping no Old Bill with his image, no way."

Gerry Phelan places a hand on her shoulder. "Stop your yakking, Miss Goalkeeper," he says quietly, "and go and get changed. It's not the boys in blue you're keeping goal for."

45

Muttering to herself, Tara leads the way to the changing-rooms.

Ten minutes later, we're warming up for the first of the three matches that will decide whether the Hotshots' involvement in the Metropolitan Cup will last longer than one evening.

We look at the other teams. Two of them look brilliant – smart kits, skilful players. The fourth team seems to be made up of skinny-legged enthusiasts like me.

Gerry Phelan gathers us round him for our final team talk.

Never mind looking at the opposition, he tells us. It's often the case that the better a team look while warming up, the weaker they are in the game itself. This pitch is going to be different to what we are used to – it has a wooden floor, we'd be using a soft ball. Most important of all, it has walls – we'll have to pass to one another by getting a deflection off the wall. For the first game, we should concentrate on getting used to the pitch and – Mr Phelan turns to Charlie and Tara – the defence should be careful not to give away any silly goals.

The manager rubs his hands as if no more needs to be said. "Oh, and Lisa – " he smiles. "Shoot on sight, OK?"

Lisa nods.

"Good luck."

As Mr Phelan and I are making our way off the pitch into the gallery, something weird happens. One of the policemen calls out as we pass, "What's the crack here,

Gerry?" The smile on his face is not what I'd call friendly.

"No crack, copper," says Mr Phelan, the colour rising to his cheeks. "Just a game of kids' football."

Sensing my curiosity, he mutters, "An old friend, Eve. We go way back."

Somehow I don't quite believe him.

The whistle blows for the first game. As the club fills with the deafening roar of supporters of the other team, St Bartholomew's School, I'm just thankful that I'm not down there on the pitch – I couldn't stand the pressure.

Nor can the players, to judge from the first two minutes. I've never seen the Hotshots play worse. It's as if they've all been given sleeping pills on toast for tea, bumping into one another, nervously tapping at the ball.

Fortunately, St Bartholomew's are even worse. Soon a hint of impatience enters the voices of their supporters.

It's not Gerry Phelan who breaks the spell – it's our only supporter. During a brief lull in the cheers for St Bartholomew's, a voice can be heard at the back of the gallery.

"Play your normal game, Hotshots! Show 'em, Lisa!"

At that moment, Tara has just rolled the ball out to Charlie. Instead of booting it out, Charlie plays it to Ellie who switches the ball across to Lisa on the right.

"More like it," Mr Phelan mutters.

Lisa has an odd habit when she's getting into her game – she appears to fall over the ball but, when she recovers her balance, it's still at her feet. Now, as the

47

voice from the back of the gallery attracts her attention, she seems to stumble. There's laughter from the crowd, but it fades quickly as Lisa recovers to shimmy past one St Bartholomew's player, then another. She's at an impossibly sharp angle to the goal when a minor miracle occurs.

"Ellie!" shouts the voice of our supporter.

Lisa looks up – and, against every selfish instinct in her body, passes the ball to Ellie.

The ball bulges the back of the St Bartholomew's net.

The rest of the game passes in a haze. Although Lisa is relaxing now, her shots on goal are unusually weak. When Gerry and I come down from the gallery at full-time, the final score is 1–0.

"It may not be enough," mutters Mr Phelan. "If two teams are equal on points, it's the goal difference which decides. We need to score more goals."

Half-listening, I'm looking for our one supporter. As the crowds clear, I see him. Sitting by himself is Jamie O'Keeffe. As I catch his eye, he looks away.

Typical Jamie. He's one of those quiet, pale boys who always look as if they have gone to bed at about two in the morning – quite possible, as it happens, because, according to Roberta, the O'Keeffe family spend most evenings watching sex and violence videos. Jamie's mum seems to be a one-woman baby farm, so that Jamie has loads of little brothers and sisters, all scrappy, scruffy and full of themselves.

For some reason, he's not like that. He has the distant, surprised look of an alien amazed to find himself on Planet Earth. There are mysteries about him – days when he never appears at school, low marks he scores although he seems quite bright – but I like him. He keeps clear of Jason and his lamebrain crew. He goes his own way.

When I join the team, Mr Phelan is addressing them in his normal quiet tones. To judge from their expressions, he is unimpressed by what he has just seen.

"Remember," he says, drawing me into the group. "We've got a substitute, so I can take any one of you off if you're not doing it for me."

I smile weakly. So being taken off to be replaced by Eve Simpson is now the ultimate threat. A knot of anger – against the manager, against my team-mates, against the world which has given me two left feet – forms in my stomach.

Anxious to hide my feelings, I look away. Near by, a group of three policemen are staring at Mr Phelan as he speaks to the team. They seem strangely amused by the sight.

The second game is better. Once again, all the support – apart from Jamie O'Keeffe – is for the other side but the Hotshots play with more determination. Tara makes a superb save within the first minute and, while the other team are still working out how they failed to go one up, Lisa has scored a simple goal at the other end. By half-time, it's 3–0 to the Hotshots and I notice Mr Phelan glancing in my direction.

No, I think, don't put me on. Not when they're doing well and I could ruin everything.

"They're playing well," I say.

"It's better." Mr Phelan nods slowly. "Are you not rarin' to go, then?"

I shake my head firmly. "Not exactly."

As it turns out, there are no more goals. Two games, two wins – surely we must be through to the next round.

Fifteen minutes later, we discover the truth. Barton Girls, the team we dismissed as wimps as they warmed up, have won both their games 3–0. Their final game is against us.

"It's very simple," Mr Phelan tells the team as the referee walks to the centre spot. "You have to win. A draw isn't enough. Play it tight in defence. Attack on the break."

The referee blows to summon the teams on to the pitch.

Mr Phelan's game plan hits problems in the second minute. Their best player, a little black girl who looks about seven but who's fast and skilful, darts past Ellie and Charlie. In her desperation to prevent a shot on goal, Roberta puts a foot inside the area. The referee's whistle is like the death-knell of the Hotshots' hopes.

A penalty.

Their striker steps up and taps the ball past Tara with contemptuous ease.

0–1. Two goals needed to avoid the end of our competition.

At first, it seems that the Hotshots will rise to the occasion. Ellie and Roberta combine to send a pass through to Ellie. Her shot misses the goal but Lisa's there for the rebound.

1–1. The hall echoes to cheers from Jamie and myself. Mr Phelan stands, hands in pockets, a vision of tense anticipation.

At half-time, fate takes a hand. On the far side of the pitch, a few latecomers squeeze through the door to see the second half of the final match.

As soon as the whistle blows for the second half, it's clear that something dramatic has happened to Lisa. She pats at the ball, prancing about like a ballerina. Normally, she's strong and direct. Not now. At one point, she loses the ball, then glances towards the doorway, flicking her hair out of her eyes.

"What the hell's she doing – ?" Mr Phelan mutters.

Then I see him. Standing by the door, square chin, long dark hair, arrogant smile. The teen dream himself has arrived.

"It's your son, Mr Phelan," I whisper.

The manager frowns. "Don't talk about my son now," he mutters. "We're just about to go out of the competition."

"But that's just it," I say desperately. "Lisa's playing for him. She's forgotten about the game. It's all Patrick's fault."

"Patrick?"

"She *fancies* him."

"Don't be daft," says Mr Phelan. Just then Lisa lets the ball go straight past her as she darts another aren't-I-cute glance in the direction of the door. "By heaven," gasps the manager. "You're right. Get ready."

"Wha—?" I jerk my head up.

"You're going on," snaps Mr Phelan.

51

"Me?" At that moment I'm thinking that, even suffering from a chronic case of true love, Lisa's of more use to the Hotshots than I'll ever be. "I can't, I —"

Mr Phelan squats down beside me and looks into my eyes. "Listen, Eve," he says quietly. "You may not be the greatest technician the game has ever seen, but you've got spirit. Go out there and show them what you can do."

Gulping, I nod.

He stands up and waves to the referee. "Sub, ref!" he yells.

The referee holds the game up.

"Lisa!" Mr Phelan says briskly. "Off!"

At any other time, it would be funny. I've never seen five players look more startled. Lisa being substituted and replaced by two-left-feet Eve? It's madness! Swinging her arms like a moody four-year-old, Lisa walks off the pitch and, without a word to me, makes her way up to the gallery.

"You've got five minutes," Mr Phelan shouts to me as I take to the pitch. "Five minutes to save the Hotshots."

As it happens, I have a couple of advantages over the other players on that pitch. I'm not tired and I have nothing to lose. It's not my fault that the Hotshots are 1–1 with five minutes to go before the last game. Once I'm on that pitch, the sound of the crowd echoing in my ears, I feel lifted by a fierce feeling of elation. It sounds stupid but somehow I know that I can save this game.

Whatever I've learnt about football – not much, admittedly – I forget for those few minutes. I don't pass the ball. I fail to talk to the other players. I don't wait until I have a clear sight of goal before shooting. I'm a coach's nightmare.

My first positive action after I come on is to bounce their best player against the wall. It's not intentional – I'm going in to tackle her and forget to put the brakes on. The referee makes a little "Calm down" gesture to me as the other girl gets to her feet. She seems to lose interest in the game after that.

Suddenly the Hotshots are alive again. I may be darting all over the pitch, this way and that, like a crazed hamster in a cage, but at least I haven't given up.

Three minutes to go. Charlie takes an optimistic long-range shot which misses by a couple of feet. I hear voices – Mr Phelan, Jamie, Patrick, even Lisa – urging us on. The other side's supporters have suddenly gone quiet.

Two minutes. Their defender passes it out to the left where their star player controls it coolly – until she sees me approaching at about a million miles an hour. For a second, perhaps remembering how hard that wall feels, she freezes. I stumble over her leg with – somehow or other – the ball in front of me. Keep going, I'm thinking, here it comes . . .

Barton Girls panic. Their defender moves across to stop me. So does their goalkeeper. Like something out of an old Charlie Chaplin film, we all arrive at the same place at the same time. There's a confused tangle of bodies just outside the Bartons' penalty area.

Seconds after the impact, I open my eyes. I cannot believe what I'm seeing. The ball is rolling slowly away from the mêlée but is just within reach of my right foot. I flick at it feebly. Slowly, slowly, the ball rolls into the net.

Goal.

Suddenly the Hotshots are all over me. It's the oddest and possibly most pathetic goal you could ever imagine but it's there.

The referee blows his whistle. Play restarts. A minute to go. By now Barton Girls have lost heart and allow us to pass the ball between us.

When the final whistle rings out, I find that for some reason I'm crying.

"It's only the first round." Gerry Phelan leans against the bar in the youth club where he has bought us all Cokes. "And you lot made heavy weather of it and all." He laughs and, for the first time since Lisa and I saw him at his flat, he seems truly happy. "I've never seen a goal like that."

"It doesn't matter how you score them," says Jamie, who has been persuaded to join us.

Lisa hobbles up to join us – mysteriously she seems to have developed a limp since the game finished.

"I was really glad you came on, Eve." She rubs the side of her leg, wincing. "This leg was getting really painful. I think I've tweaked a hamstring."

"Tweaked a heartstring more like," Charlie mutters under her breath.

"Probably reaching for that last goal of mine." Lisa's continuing her little routine. "Oh well, at least I'm the team's top scorer." She flashes a smile in Patrick's direction, but Mr Teenage Hunk seems more interested in a policeman who's talking to Gerry. It's the constable who spoke to us earlier.

"Hotshots, eh, Gerry?"

Mr Phelan looks away.

"Your idea for a name, was it?" continues the policeman. He looks down at us. "Gerry here was always very interested in . . . . hot items."

Mr Phelan steps forward and, for a moment, seems to lose control. There's a dangerous look in his eye which I've never seen before.

"Dad!" says Patrick sharply.

Draining his Coke, Mr Phelan walks wordlessly to the door.

We follow uncertainly. "What was all that about?" Tara whispers.

"Not sure," I say. "But I have a feeling that we haven't heard the last of it."

CHAPTER FOUR

Fancy Footwork

"**T**he loser now will be later to win."

Roberta, Tara and I are standing in the corridor at breaktime the next day when Mr Morley breezes up to us, singing one of his songs.

"Sorry, sir?" goes Roberta.

"I hear congratulations are in order," says the head-teacher. "Rumour has it that you did yourselves proud last night."

"We're in the Area Finals," says Roberta.

"Great." Mr Morley drops his voice confidentially. "I'm looking for ways to allow you to train in the playground." He actually winks at us. "And it would probably be a good idea for you to wear the school kit next time."

"I thought we were banned." Tara blunders in with her normal elephantine tact.

But Mr Morley isn't taking incoming messages. "Two teams in the Area Finals." A distant, dreamy look has entered his eyes. "I don't think Broadhurst has ever managed that before."

"What about Mr Phelan?" I ask. "Is it all right for him to be our manager now?"

"I'll ponder," says Mr Morley airily. "I'm sure we can work something out." He bustles off in the direction of the staff room.

"We're not changing our strip, no way," says Tara. "They may have been torn and smelt of old cabbages but those purple shirts brought us luck."

There's an odd atmosphere at our next practice. We should be united, confident, but a strange sense of anti-climax is in the air. Gerry Phelan seems quiet, distracted. Tara's as noisy and disruptive as only she can be.

Strangest of all is Lisa. Her hamstring has miraculously become untweaked (big surprise) but she's fallen back into her old habits – never passing the ball, treating the game as if it's a Lisa Show-off Benefit, going through a big pantomime of frustration every time anyone else makes a mistake.

Occasionally I glance over to Mr Phelan, hoping he'll say something to her, but he stands on the touchline, hands sunk deep in his pockets, following the game with unseeing eyes.

After the practice, I walk home with Charlie.

"It's crazy," she says. "Lisa's moods seem to affect the whole team. When she's up, we're smiling. When she's down, everything goes to pieces. Why can't we just ignore her? Everyone knows she's just a drama queen."

"It's not even as if she's our most important player," I say quietly.

"Eh?" Charlie laughs in surprise.

"You are," I tell her. "Lisa may have the fancy footwork, Tara may make all the noise, but it's you, standing there in defence, who keeps the team together."

"You reckon." Charlie looks away, almost impatiently. I've noticed this about her – she's uneasy with compliments. "Here's how I see the problem, right," she says, changing the subject away from herself. "Lisa was really thrown by what happened on Tuesday. It showed that we could win without her. Somehow we've got to give her back her confidence."

"I've always thought that Lisa has the most confidence of us all."

Charlie shakes her head.

"She's a mess. I reckon she pretends to be more grown-up than she is because she's trying to be like her mum. Underneath it all she's really insecure – that's why she always has to prove herself."

"Deep." I smile at Charlie. "Very deep."

"Shut up, Eve. Are you going to her party on Saturday?"

"Party?" To tell the truth, this is the first I've heard of any party. "Yeah, I'll be there. What time is it?"

"Seven onwards. Her mum's away for the night, I think. Got a new boyfriend apparently."

"Her mum? This time last week she was dying of a broken heart."

Charlie shrugs. "It's like Lisa's leg. They mend quickly in that family."

A party with no parents. What could be better?

Yet Saturday round at Lisa's turns out to be a surprise.

It's the perfect set-up. Mrs Martin is away for the weekend (a health farm being the latest excuse) and Lisa's seventeen-year-old brother Josh is supposed to be baby-sitting. Of course, Josh has other plans and won't be seen until the football appears on television on Sunday afternoon. Leaving us free. The perfect family arrangement really.

Lisa has asked Charlie, Tara, Roberta and (after a few hints) me to sleep over. A few other friends, she says casually, might drop by during the evening.

And here's the surprise. We're just lolling around in front of the television, pigging out on crisps and Coke, when at about nine o'clock, the front doorbell rings.

Tara looks through the window as Lisa goes to answer the door.

"Oh *lame*," she goes. "It's only Jason, Dominic and Stevie."

We look at one another in amazement. So much for our relaxed evening among friends.

"Yo." The two boys wander in, trying to look cool. To be fair, they're a bit smarter than usual. Dominic's done something unusual to his hair – washed it maybe – and Jason looks almost human.

Almost, but not quite.

Stevie stands beside Lisa at the door, chewing hard. "What you watching, guys?" she asks.

"Nothing much," I mutter, making space for her on the sofa. Stevie wanders over and slumps down beside me. I'm thinking to myself, Make yourself at home, why don't you?

"There's this ace movie on the other channel. Patrick Swayze. I saw it in the States."

For a moment, there's an embarrassed silence as Jason and Dominic edge towards the TV. Neither of them has quite the nerve to sit down yet.

"So." Stevie looks around brightly. "What d'you say we switch over?"

Tara shrugs. "Don't mind us."

We watch this so-called ace movie for about two minutes. Then Stevie says, almost to herself, "I guess you guys feel pretty bad about the news, huh?"

"What news is that, Stevie?" I ask.

Lisa, who's been busying about the kitchen, appears at the door with a big bowl of crisps in her hand. "Could we talk about that some other time?" she says with a nervous toss of her black hair.

"Jeez, Steve." Jason's glaring at Stevie. "You and your big mouth."

Stevie acts surprised. "Well, excuse me," she says. "I thought that was the whole idea of this party. Like, be friends in spite of everything, right?"

"Shut up be friends," mutters Tara.

"Yeah." Dominic clears his throat. "We just thought that, since we're all in the Area Finals of the Met, we should work together."

"Yeah, help each other out," Lisa mumbles into the crisps. It doesn't take a genius to see that something is going on here.

Roberta smiles cheerfully. "I'll go for that. It was dead boring having only Jamie O'Keeffe supporting us."

"That malco." Jason grins at Dominic. "Just because he couldn't get into our team."

"Jamie's all right," I say. "He's been loyal to us when no one else was."

"Come *on*, you guys," Stevie sits forward in the sofa. "Why does no one in this country ever say what they mean? Are you going to tell them, Lisa, or shall I?"

Lisa turns off the television and stands in front of it, like someone who's been asked to make a speech.

"Erm, right." She gives a quick fake grin, possibly her most annoying gesture. "It's like this. I have been approached by Mr Armstrong, the manager of the boys' team. Apparently they need a striker. They want – " She paused dramatically. "Well, they want *moi*."

"Shut up they want you," says Tara automatically.

"But you aren't a boy." Roberta's smiling, as if this is some joke she doesn't quite understand. "You don't look remotely like a boy."

"Doesn't matter." Jason speaks up at last. "Under the rules of the Met Cup, there's a general competition and a girls' competition. You can change members of a team for the general competition so long as they belong to the same school."

"We definitely need a goalscorer," goes Dominic. "We could use Lisa's pace."

"So could we," says Roberta. "What about the Hotshots?"

"I'll join your team." Stevie speaks up. "You've seen me play. I'm not so terrible."

"I get it." I manage to find my voice at last. "It wasn't your cousin who rang the other day, was it? You were hatching your little plan." Dominic and Lisa look shifty. "Anyway, Morley's not going to allow this."

Lisa gives a stagey little wince. "Erm, not true," she says. "Mr Armstrong has discussed it with the Head. They both decided that it would be really good for girls' sport at Broadhurst if a girl appeared in the boys' team. You know – break down the barriers."

And, yes, I can just about see that. Of course Morley would buy this line – the way he'd see it was as great publicity for the school, another blow struck against sexism.

Tara's on her feet, her normally pale features flushed with anger. "Since when has betraying your friends been good for girls' sport? You're just a traitor."

"Cool it, Tara." Stevie looks embarrassed now, as if she wishes she had never raised the subject.

"Shut up cool it," shouts Tara.

"Don't you see what's happening here, Lisa?" Although Charlie speaks quietly, everyone turns to listen to her. "What they're saying is that it's more important how the boys do in the Met Cup than the girls. When they do sport, it matters. With us, it's just a bit of fun. Joining the boys might be good for you. It may even get a few headlines for Morley and the school but, the fact is, it's just the same old sexist story."

"I haven't finally decided," says Lisa weakly. "I said I'd let Mr Armstrong know after the weekend. My mother thinks I should go with the boys."

"That figures," says Roberta quietly.

"You go beyond, Lisa." Tara's striding up and down, angrily twisting an empty Coke can in her hand.

"Have you discussed this with Patrick?" I ask, a rather brilliant idea taking shape in my mind.

"That creep." Lisa turns to switch the television on. "What could he tell me?"

"He's good on this sort of thing. He's very . . . wise."

A tragic, distant look has come into Lisa's eyes. "He doesn't even return my calls."

"Well, I'm off," goes Tara, throwing the mangled Coke can on to the floor. "I'm not staying here tonight, no way." She walks to the door.

"I'll let you all know on Monday," says Lisa.

Charlie gets to her feet. "And we'll let you know, Lisa. Maybe we won't want to play with you. This changes everything." She glances at Roberta and me. "You coming?"

Wondering how exactly I'm going to explain to my parents why I've decided not to stay with Lisa, I follow Charlie to the door.

"Sheesh, this is embarrassing," Stevie's muttering as we leave the room. "I'm sorry, guys," she calls out after us.

"D'you want to stay with me?" Roberta asks as we close the door behind us.

I shake my head. "No, I'd better get back. I have a call to make."

"Call?" Charlie looks surprised. "Are you up to something, Eve?"

"Maybe."

We make our way home in thoughtful silence.

"Patrick? It's Eve – Eve Simpson."

"Oh, hi, Eve. Great to hear from you. Dad's not in right now."

"Actually, it was you I needed to talk to."

"Me?"

"We have a problem which you can help us with. All it will take is just one call and a bit of charm and persuasion . . ."

It's a low-down, dirty trick – of course it is – but I'm not going to let all our hopes, and all Mr Phelan's work, go down the drain because of Lisa Martin's giant ego. All's fair in love, war and football, is what I say. So I use Mr Supercool himself. And, because he's a good son who knows how important the Hotshots are to his father, Mr Supercool co-operates.

There's a sort of head-in-the-clouds wooziness to Lisa when she comes into school on Monday. She stares into space during the first two lessons, doodling on her exercise books.

"Well?" asks Tara, as the Hotshots gather around her desk at breaktime.

"Well, what?" says Lisa vaguely.

"What's your decision?"

"Oh, that." Lisa runs her finger around the edge of her notebook, milking the moment for a few more seconds of attention. "Um, I'm staying. Hotshots for ever, that's what I say."

"Definitely?" This is Roberta, who knows that Lisa's mind can change just like the wind. "No going back?"

"Definitely." Lisa stands up. "I've been given advice by a certain person and that certain person thinks I should stick with you guys."

She wanders out of the classroom, humming contentedly to herself.

"She's too much, that one," goes Roberta.

"I wonder who the certain person was," says Tara.

"Guess." Ellie holds up Lisa's notebook. It has been decorated with neatly drawn hearts.

And, for just the very briefest of moments, I feel almost guilty.

There have been times when I've wished that, if there's such a thing as reincarnation, that I could come back to earth as Lisa Martin – pretty, athletic, strong, self-assured. This week is not one of those times.

She's like an emotional roller-coaster.

A few days ago, she's down because of her performance in the Met Cup.

Then she's up when the boys approach her about joining the team.

Then she's down when the Hotshots tell her that she's being a traitor.

Then she's up when Patrick rings her.

Then she's down when Patrick doesn't ring her again.

Her mother is not exactly a steadying influence. Mrs

Martin's weekend at the "health farm" turns out to have been a disaster. For the past few days, there have been tears, sulks, late-night telephone calls. From what Lisa tells us, the soap opera of her home life is going through a particularly rough stage.

Luckily for us, she leaves all her troubles on the touchline when it comes to football practice. As if the dramatic events of the past weekends have unified us in some strange way, the Hotshots play better than ever during the practices the following week.

Gerry Phelan has taken to putting our strikers and midfield on one side and our defence, including me, on the other. We're evenly matched and a new sense of quiet professionalism takes over during our games.

Lisa herself is back at her best, learning new skills and tricks from Gerry. Sometimes during a game, she falls back in defence, gathers the ball and simply runs at the opposition. Then, when they get used to that, she'll chip the ball diagonally across the pitch so that it lands with a cunning backspin at the feet of Roberta or Ellie.

Suddenly I can see why the boys were so keen to recruit her.

They see it, too. Jason and some of his friends have taken to hanging around outside the wire fence during our practice games. There are no mocking jokes now — it's as if they have suddenly realized that we're not just a bunch of girls fooling around, but that we're a team.

Every practice, Stevie is among the boys, watching us train. Sometimes I catch a look of envy in her eyes and I think back to that night at Lisa's house. It was Stevie who made the boys and Lisa face up to what was going on. She may be a bit loud sometimes but there's an openness about her which I like.

"Nice shot, Eve," she shouts when I take one of my rare pokes at goal.

"Thanks, Stevie." I smile.

It's three weeks now to the Area Finals, and I can't believe that things are going this well.

Too well.

The following Tuesday, when I return from school, my mother greets me with an unusually glum expression on her face.

"We have a problem," she says, passing me a brown envelope with her name scrawled in childish writing on the front.

Inside is a photocopy of a newspaper cutting. The lead story's headlined "FORMER FOOTBALL HERO JAILED". At first I don't recognize the slight, long-haired figure in the photograph beside the piece. Then I see the name on the caption.

"Gerry Phelan." I sit down slowly on a kitchen chair. Slowly, carefully, I read the news item.

Former footballing star Gerald Phelan had squandered talent, money and opportunity to turn to a life of petty crime, Acton Crown Court was told today. Phelan, tipped by experts as a future international before a serious knee injury ended his career two years ago, was accused of having received stolen goods over a period of eighteen months.

Phelan's solicitor had argued for clemency, pointing out that he had no previous convictions. "This young man suffered a terrible disappointment when forced to give up a promising career," Mr Peter Tucker pointed out. *As a professional footballer, he had developed a taste for the good life and had become addicted to gambling. "He turned to crime as a desperate measure to avoid the shame of bankruptcy,"* the court was told.

Rejecting the defence's argument, magistrates pointed out that Phelan had set an appalling example to youngsters who supported him as a footballer. A custodial sentence of two years was imposed.

Phelan's wife Mary, who is six months pregnant, had to be helped from the court.

"How did you get this?" I ask my mother.

She passes me a note scrawled on a scrap of lined paper. It reads, "WOULD YOU TRUST THIS MAN WITH YOUR DAUGHTER?"

"But this must have happened ages ago," I say weakly. "Look at the photograph."

"Sixteen years," says Mum. "I rang Mr Morley as soon as it came." She nods in the direction of the note. "He'd been sent one of these too. Tara's dad had just rung him."

"But who'd do this to Gerry?"

"That's not really the point, is it?" my mother says briskly. "The fact is he's been in jail and now he's in charge of a group of schoolgirls."

"So what? That has nothing to do with stolen goods. Anyway, it all happened sixteen years ago. What did the head say?"

"He's going to talk to Mr Phelan. One of the teachers is prepared to take you to the next round."

"I bet." In spite of myself, I have to laugh. "Now that we're in the Area Finals, they'll be falling over themselves to volunteer."

"I wonder who has it in for him," my mother murmurs.

The telephone rings. It's Tara, caught between excitement at the dramatic news and concern about the Hotshots.

"No way is Gerry going to be allowed to manage us," she repeats several times. "He's gone ridiculously beyond. No way."

"What do your parents think?"

"Dad's climbing the walls." Tara lowers her voice slightly. "Anybody would think Gerry was a murderer or something."

As Tara rants on, I find myself wondering which of the Hotshots' parents would stick by Mr Phelan. Lisa's mum will do what she's told by Lisa. I don't know Charlie's parents but, from the way they fuss about her, I imagine they're pretty strict. Roberta's mum and dad are separated but seem reasonably sane, as do Ellie's. As for my own parents – I glance across the room at Mum – I can probably convince them. They may be old-fashioned worriers where their only daughter is concerned, they may be a bit iffy about the whole idea of girls' football, but fairness is one of their golden rules. And Mr Phelan getting dumped for something that happened sixteen years ago is not exactly fair.

My mind's made up. "If Mr Phelan's out, I'm not playing any more," I tell Tara during a brief lull in her monologue.

"Shut up you're not playing any more," she snaps. "What about the Area Finals? We'll be in the local paper and everything."

"I don't care. It was Mr Phelan who got us there. I'm out." I pause. "How about you, Tara?"

For a moment, there's silence. The Hotshots can live with my departure but if I can just persuade Tara to join me, Mr Morley will have to take notice.

"It's not that I care about him breaking the law," says Tara, a wheedling note in her voice. "But it's Dad. He says Gerry's evil."

"And I suppose he's never been in trouble," I say sharply.

"Anyway, I don't think Gerry would want us to give up," says Tara changing the subject.

"It's the principle."

Tara sighs and goes into her normal swearing routine. It's not exactly her style to make decisions on the basis of principles.

"We've got to stick together," I plead. "That's how we've always done it so far. United – on the pitch and off."

"I was really looking forward to that game," Tara says miserably.

"And we can still play it. Don't you see? Imagine how it would look for the school if we withdrew from the Cup now. Maybe we could ring the papers about it."

"What about our parents?"

"Who's playing the football, us or them?" I say decisively. "You ring Lisa and Charlie. I'll get on to Ellie and Roberta. All right?"

Tara mumbles a few half-hearted protests.

"You're great, Tara," I say. "Talk to you in a minute."

As I put down the phone, I catch my mother smiling at me.

"What a little stirrer you've turned out to be," she says quietly.

"I'm right though, aren't I, Mum? I know you don't like me playing football but we can't allow them to sack our manager just because he got into trouble years ago."

"What's he like, this Phelan man?"

I tell her about the visit Lisa and I paid to his flat. "It's true he drinks a bit but he's always been fine when he's taken the game. He's brought Patrick up on his own for the past five years – he can't be that bad."

My mother sighs. "I'll talk to your father about it."

That's good enough for me.

Just before supper, the telephone rings again. Luckily, it's me who picks it up. The slurred voice of Gerry Phelan comes on the line.

"I know what you're doing, Eve," he says unsteadily. "Charlie just rang me." I hear the clink of glass as he drawls, "Just do us this one little favour will you . . . Play the Area Finals . . . Do what the school wants . . . Forget old Phelan . . . he's finished."

"Tara and I are speaking to the team. We're agreed on this. We want you as manager."

"Play!" Mr Phelan shouts so loudly that I glance across the sitting-room to where my father is reading the newspaper. "Loyalty's for idiots, Eve."

"We'll see the head in the morning," I say coolly. "Maybe we shouldn't practise tomorrow – until it's sorted."

"Practise." Mr Phelan gives a long, weary sigh. "Got to practise. Go to the park as usual."

"All right," I say unenthusiastically.

"You're a good girl, Eve," Mr Phelan murmurs.

"Just don't call Mr Morley," I tell him. "Leave this to us."

"You're a good, brave, kind – "

I hang up.

My father's staring at me with undisguised curiosity.

"Mr Phelan," I say.

"How's he taking it?"

I nod slowly. This is one white lie that it's impossible to avoid. "Pretty good," I say.

Looking at us as we hover outside Mr Morley's study at breaktime the next morning, you'd think we were the ones discovered to have had a jail sentence and a drink problem. Apart from Tara, who's her usual loud self, we're all edgy and nervous. Between us, I was hoping a sort of tough team spirit would help us weather the storm that's on its way, but right now we look about as tough as a blancmange melting in the summer sun.

"Ah." Mr Morley opens the study door. "A deputation." He makes an odd waving motion like a bored traffic cop and we troop into his office. "Somehow I thought you might like to see me. It will be about your manager."

We stand awkwardly in front of Mr Morley's desk as he fusses with a few papers in front of him like a man who really has more important problems to deal with. "Well?" He looks up sharply.

We have agreed that Lisa should be our spokesperson. Not only is she captain of the Hotshots, but she has always been good at using her charm to get her own way.

"We just wanted to say that we think Mr Phelan is a brilliant manager," she says hesitantly. "If it wasn't for him, we would have got nowhere."

The headteacher puts his fingers together and purses his lips as he considers this brilliant, insightful and profound speech. As another silence settles on the room, it occurs to me that he's actually taking pleasure in this situation. Perhaps that's why people become headteachers. They actually enjoy life's little dramas – particularly when they always have the leading role.

"Thank you, Lisa," he says, frowning thoughtfully and staring at his fingertips. "I appreciate what you have to say and frankly it redounds to your credit that you have been so loyal to Gerry Phelan. I'm thoroughly . . . impressed."

All around me, I can sense the resolution draining from my team-mates as the Head gives us the old, old flattery line.

"Now because you've been so adult about this," he

continues, "I'm going to be very direct and straight with you. I had my doubts about Gerry Phelan when he first appeared, as you know. Since then he's done a marvellous job with you – " his smile covers all six of us – "you Hotshots."

Don't fall for this, I'm thinking to myself.

"But" – a heavy, world-weary sigh – "we all have a problem, don't we?" He looks up with a phony, guys-together smile. "And it's a serious problem. As head-teacher, I'm responsible to your parents and the governors. If anything should happen, there would be serious repercussions not only for you and your parents, but for the school."

"Yeah, but what could happen – ?" Tara starts in but is silenced by a glacial look from Mr Morley.

"So here's what we're going to do," he says in a quiet, authoritative voice. "Mr Phelan is very welcome to continue with the Hotshots" – another dramatic pause – "but only as a supporter. From today, you will be under supervision of a member of staff. Despite her mishap" – Morley smiles tolerantly in the general direction of Roberta – "Miss Wilson has agreed to take up the reins once more. Obviously she will consult Mr Phelan on matters of . . . soccer tactics."

There's another awkward silence as we consider this idea. I try to imagine a conversation about tactics between Miss Wilson and Gerry Phelan. It's got to be a joke.

"I hope you'll all agree that this is a compromise acceptable to all concerned," says the headteacher in an

I'm-now-closing-this-discussion tone of voice. "All right?"

"Would Mr Phelan be able to come to all the matches?" Lisa asks.

"Of course."

"And there won't be any sort of public announcement about him not being manager?"

"No. That would be insensitive. With your help, I'd like to finesse this little problem so that no one's hurt. Now – " Mr Morley stands up and rubs his hands. "I've got to make a couple of telephone calls so unless there's anything else, we'll regard the matter as closed. I'm very glad that you've – "

"No."

I'm taking a deep breath to make my own speech but it's not me who steps forward, but Charlie. Her eyes are blazing with anger.

"I beg your pardon, Charlie?" The smile has left Mr Morley's face.

"It's just unfair," goes Charlie. "You're still punishing a man for something he did sixteen years ago. Whenever you talk to us in Assembly, you're always going on about justice, about sticking up for people who are less lucky than you. You've told us that, if there's one thing you hate, it's a bully. Well, this is bullying Mr Phelan."

I smile to myself as Charlie's speaking. She can be quite impressive when she wants to be. It's as if the world – Mr Morley, teachers, parents, the boys' team – are no more than a strike force advancing on the goal behind her. And there stands Charlie – big, strong, unwavering, apparently without any fear. I suppose that, being black, Charlie understands better than the rest of us how to fight life's everyday injustices.

Mr Morley writhes uncomfortably in his chair. "I hardly think that – "

"Yeah," says Tara, changing her mind yet again. "That's right."

"I am merely suggesting to you that a former criminal is hardly the right person to be in charge of a group of children," says Mr Morley irritably.

"The point is, sir," I speak in my most reasonable voice, "Mr Phelan's done nothing wrong so far as the school or the Metropolitan Cup is concerned."

"If you do this, the Hotshots will refuse to play," says Charlie.

"You mean *you* will refuse to play, Charlie," says the headteacher.

"None of us will play," says Lisa, and it's all I can do not to hug her with gratitude, right there and then. Of all of us, Lisa is the one who cares most about playing in the Met Cup. She's turned down the chance of playing with the boys. "We're all agreed about this," she says.

Mr Morley walks quickly to the door.

"So be it," he says, showing us out. "Clearly I was wrong to think you'd take an adult view of the situation. Let me know if you change your mind. Otherwise I'll tell the organizers of the Metropolitan Cup that Broadhurst Comprehensive is withdrawing the team. Furthermore I'll speak to each of your parents to ensure that none of you associates with Phelan again.

The question of individual detentions will also have to be considered."

Miserably, we shuffle out of the study.

"So much for standing up for principles," sighs Ellie, as we make our way slowly back to the class-room.

"Even if we're out, at least we've shown that the Hotshots can't be pushed around," says Charlie.

"Yeah. Hotshot power," says Tara, and suddenly we're all smiling at one another. Each of us in our heart knows that, whatever happens now, we've done the right thing.

"Gerry wanted us to practise in the park after school," I say.

"What's the point?" asks Ellie.

"The point is to show that they haven't won," says Charlie. "Anyway Morley might change his mind."

"And pigs might fly." A cloud seems to have settled over Lisa once more.

I put a hand on her shoulder. "You have to stand up for these things, eh, Lisa," I say quietly.

"Get you, football's answer to Mother Theresa," she mumbles gloomily.

It's a hot day, too hot for thinking, too hot for football – but, in spite of the weather and Mr Morley, we all turn up for practice in the park that afternoon.

When we reach the park, there, in our normal practice place, is a tall, long-haired figure, juggling a football from one foot to another.

"It's Patrick," says Tara. "Hey, Lisa, dreamboat's back in town."

"Hm?" Lisa looks away in a pathetic attempt to hide her blushes.

Patrick flicks the ball up and catches it as we approach.

"You're late," he says, as if he were a real grown-up coach or something. "Let's start with some fitness exercises."

And, amazingly, there isn't a murmur of dissent. Patrick may look as if he should be striding along a Californian beach with a surfboard under his arm and blonde airheads fainting as he passes by, but right now he has the sort of authority that we're looking for.

Of course, Tara tries it on with a few muttered remarks about Lisa, but soon even she gives up and concentrates on training. It's a good practice. On the pitch at least, the Hotshots are playing well.

As usual, I spend some of the game in goal. As I watch Charlie defending me against anyone who dares come within ten yards of the penalty area, I can't help thinking over the events of the day.

For a start, who's behind the campaign to discredit Mr Phelan? One of his enemies or ours? The better the Hotshots do as a team, the more people seem to stand in the way of our success. Miss Wilson, Mr Armstrong, any one of the teachers at Broadhurst, Jason and his gang – they all have reasons to be jealous. Then there's Gerry – some of the policemen we met at the youth club weren't exactly friendly towards him.

Anyway, discovering who sent out that old cutting was unlikely to make the headteacher change his mind. There's no avoiding the fact that we need help from some parents.

Something strange happens to my father when friends of mine come round to the house. He becomes skittish and makes bad jokes, as if he's read somewhere that the way to get children on your side is to be a bit childish yourself. It's embarrassing, to tell the truth – like watching a bad comedian on television.

Relax, Dad, I've always wanted to say. Just be your normal, grumpy self.

"Wow, a major Hotshot delegation," he goes as we troop into the house after the practice in the park. "What an honour."

Mum appears at the top of the stairs. "I hope you're not all expecting to eat. I've only got – "

"We need some advice," I say, leading everyone into the sitting-room.

My father follows, then slumps down on a chair. "Sure," he says, hooking a leg over the arm of the chair in a relaxed-dad sort of way. "Shoot."

It has been agreed that Lisa should do the talking. Deep down within my father's soul is a slumbering good guy who, in another age, has marched, protested, sung, "We shall not be moved" to the strains of a guitar. If anyone can awaken this champion of peace and justice, it's Lisa with her wild hair, her flashing eyes, her way of dramatizing everything.

"We believe that Mr Phelan is the victim of moral blackmail and police corruption," she says, using the two phrases which I have fed her on the walk back to the house.

"Yeah," says my father. "It certainly sounds as if he has been stitched up royally."

"We went to see Mr Morley this morning," Lisa continues. "We told him that, if Mr Phelan goes, we go."

"Solidarity." For a moment, I think Dad's going to raise a clenched fist but he seems to think better of it and runs his fingers through his wispy hair. "What did he say?"

"He doesn't seem to care." Lisa's voice cracks tragically. This is a truly great dramatic performance. "He called Mr Phelan a criminal. Everybody seems to be against us."

Before my eyes, I see my parents' view of the Hotshots changing. Until now, they have been unenthusiastic, convinced that playing football was about to change their sweet, twinkle-toed only daughter into a foul-mouthed cavegirl whose knuckles drag along the floor. As Lisa speaks, we're becoming a heroic cause worth fighting for. Vietnam, the Bomb – and now the Hotshots.

"We've got to make him change his mind, Mr Simpson," Charlie's saying. "We've worked really hard to get to the Area Finals."

"You certainly have," says Dad. "We've been really impressed by what you girls have done."

Somehow I manage to swallow back my protests.

80

"What do we do, Mr Simpson?" Lisa asks. "Should we get everyone in the school to sign a petition?"

"Yeah," goes Roberta. "A Save the Hotshots Appeal."

"No." Mum has been standing at the door, smiling at Lisa's impassioned performance. "I don't think that will work. After all, Mr Morley hasn't banned the Hotshots. He's only told you to get a new manager."

"No, Morley's a politician," says my father. "He won't worry about what the children say – "

"No way," mutters Tara.

"But he might worry about the parents. The first thing to do is to activate them. Each of you should get your mum or dad to write a letter tonight, supporting Gerry Phelan."

I look around. Already Tara and Roberta are looking worried at this idea of parent activation.

"Ask them to point out that it was Gerry Phelan who managed the team into the Area Finals, that he's done nothing reprehensible while managing the team, and that to deprive him of managership on the grounds of tittle-tattle from another child's parents is a gross abrogation of – "

"Morley won't listen," I say quickly. If my father thinks that delivering one of his speeches about reprehensible abrogations is going to help, he's misunderstood what life is like in other families.

"And why not, Eve?" he asks coldly.

"Dad, he's used to fobbing off parents. You say that he worries about what they think of him, but he doesn't care."

"You should see how he talks to my mother," mutters Charlie.

"Right." My father frowns and moves into deep thought mode for a few moments. "Plan B. We leak the story to the local press and get a local campaign going to put pressure on Mr Morley. After all, the Hotshots are representing the whole area in the team. Now it just so happens that a friend of mine works on the *Gazette*."

"Forget it, Matthew," says my mother with a hint of impatience in her voice. "It's difficult enough to get Clive out of the pub for a murder, let alone a girls' football team."

"I'm not sure that – "

"You need to ring up Judith Fairbrother and the Reverend Pardew."

My father writhes uncomfortably in his chair.

"I really think this is a matter for the governors," says Mum.

"I wonder about that."

It doesn't take a genius to see that the idea of contacting these great pillars of the community to discuss the case of an Irish ex-footballer with a jail record and a drink problem is rather less than appealing to my father.

"This really is important to us, Mr Simpson," says Lisa with deep sincerity.

"I agree with Lisa," says Mum. "If Morley gets away with this, it sets an appalling example to the children."

My father sighs and fidgets with a copy of the *Guardian* lying near by. "I need to mull this over," he

82

says, darting an irritated look in my mother's direction. "I'll talk to the governors – but I need to do it my way, all right?"

"Thanks, Mr Simpson." Lisa flashes her most dazzling smile. "Eve said we could rely on you to help."

"She did, did she?"

I shrug innocently.

"Best be on my way," says Tara. "I need to catch my dad before he goes out playing snooker – he's got a letter to write."

"That's a good point," says Lisa as the Hotshots make their way from the sitting-room to the hall. "My mum's got a date tonight."

"You could fake her handwriting like you did before," says Ellie.

"Fake? Me?" As I close the front door behind them, the raucous voices of the Hotshots fade.

"Honestly." My father stands in the hall playing one of his favourite roles, the put-upon male. "Whatever happened to girlish charm?"

"Well, I think it's great to see girls with a bit of confidence," says my mother. "Your Mr Phelan must be a good manager."

Dad gives a rueful little laugh as he looks at me. "Another fine mess you've got me into, young woman."

"Thanks, Dad."

"No promises," he says.

CHAPTER FIVE

Swings and Roundabouts

Who will crack?
Whose nerve, now that it seems that the Hotshots are on their own, will break first?

Lisa Martin's, right?

Wrong.

The next day, Lisa arrives at school with a letter from her mother, protesting in red ink and in prose shrieking with CAPITALS and !!!! marks, about the treatment of Gerry Phelan. It's too authentically hysterical for Lisa to have faked it.

Somehow I doubt whether Mr Morley will be too impressed by Mrs Martin's arguments. On the other hand, the fact that the parents of all but one of the team have written to express their support of Mr Phelan might just make him think twice about his decision.

The missing parents are Mr and Mrs Williams, Tara's mum and dad. In fact, it's not just their letter that's missing – Tara doesn't show up for school that day.

As soon as I get home after school, I telephone her.

"She's not back yet, Eve," her mother tells me.

"Back?"

"Yeah. She's not back from school. She seems to be a bit late today."

"Ah." I decide to keep quiet. "Right. Fine."

Problem.

It doesn't take long for me to ring round to muster a search party. Telling my mother that we have a football practice, I leave for the park where I meet up with Lisa, Charlie, Roberta and Ellie at the playground.

"Tara's run away from home," I tell them. "She left for school as usual this morning."

"It's that letter," says Charlie. "On her way back from your house last night, she told us her father would never agree to it. Apparently he's taken against Gerry for some reason."

"She's always fighting with him anyway," says Roberta.

This is true. Within seconds of being in Tara's house, you discover that she and Mr Williams are not exactly twin souls.

"We've got to find her," I mutter. "Before she gets into real trouble."

After a bit of discussion, it's agreed that Roberta, Ellie and Lisa will go to the youth club that Tara belongs to. Charlie and I will look down the High Street.

We're in luck. Coming out of a clothes shop (what else?), we see Stevie.

"Hey, guys," she goes. "Guess who I just saw."

"We haven't got time for games," Charlie tells her.

"Yeah, right." With a shrug, Stevie turns to walk away. "Just thought you might like to know that your goalkeeper is hanging out at a fairground down the road."

"Stevie!" I call after her. "Tell us where down the road. This is an emergency."

She hesitates, then wanders back to where Charlie and I are standing. "OK." She nods. "It's in Westcroft Park. I'll show you."

As we walk quickly down the High Street, then through a complicated network of back streets, I realize that we should have thought of the fair before. Tara's a sucker for the roundabouts and big wheel and candy-floss. Whenever there was a visiting fair in our area, she'd be down there. Where better to disappear for a day?

Westcroft Park is a small square of land surrounded by shops. Because it's a fine evening, the place is thronging with children, teenagers and the occasional parent.

"Should we split up?" I shout over the din of the music.

"Let's stick together," says Charlie, sensible as usual.

Five minutes later, we've found Tara. She's standing by a rifle range, looking even wilder and grimier than she usually does. In front of her is a tall uniformed police officer. Wherever Tara happens to be, trouble is never far behind.

For a moment we hang back, uncertain as to what to do. Then, to my amazement, Stevie steps forward and takes the initiative.

"Hi there, Tara!" she says brightly. "Sorry I'm late."
Tara looks at us guardedly.

"Do you know this young lady?" the policeman asks
Stevie suspiciously.

"Why, sure," Stevie trills. "We agreed to meet here.
It's the first time I've ever been to one of your English
fairgrounds."

"Is it now?" The policeman nods slowly.

"Is something wrong, officer?" Stevie, in her smart
designer clothes and with that shucks-I'm-just-a-tourist
smile on her face, looks a picture of innocence.

"Wrong? Only that she's been hanging around here
all afternoon," says the policeman. "Hasn't got a penny
in her pocket."

Stevie looks surprised. "You guys have to *pay* policemen?" She reaches into the pocket of her blue designer
tracksuit and pulls out a couple of notes. "How much
do I owe you?"

I glance at Charlie nervously. This girl has real
style.

"It's not for me," says the policeman irritably. "And
if you think you can bribe me – "

"She's American," I interrupt quickly, but the man
has turned back to Tara.

"If I see you round here once more." He holds a
threatening finger an inch from her face. "You'll be
down to the station so fast that your feet won't touch
the ground."

"Suit yourself," mutters Tara, glancing away casually.

With a baleful look in Stevie's direction, the policeman wanders off.

"Let's get out of here," says Charlie. For once, Tara follows without complaint.

"I was going to run away with them," she says moodily. "If you hadn't come along, I'd have been working on the roundabouts. Good job, that."

"If we hadn't come along, you'd have been arrested," says Charlie angrily.

"Shut up arrested."

"OK, guys, I'll leave you to it," says Stevie as we emerge from the park. "I gotta get home. I'm late."

Charlie smiles. "Cool work, Stevie," she says.

"Yeah thanks, Stevie," I go.

"You're very welcome." Stevie does a comical little bow and skips off down the street.

"Bloomin' Yank," mutters Tara.

With some difficulty, we persuade Tara to return home. Just possibly her parents haven't discovered that she bunked off school, I tell her as we head for the High Street. And so what if her dad has a bit of a thing about Gerry Phelan?

"Bit of a thing!" Tara shouts. "He hates him. He loathes him. He goes ridiculously beyond – he wishes Gerry was dead. Shut up bit of a thing."

After this explosion, we walk on in silence for a bit.

"Bloody child abuser," Tara says suddenly.

"Gerry?" Charlie looks shocked.

"My father." Tara's pulling up the sleeve of her T-shirt. It takes a while but she finds a small bruise near the shoulder. She points at it, like an old soldier showing a war wound. "That's where he grabbed me last night. I'll grass him up to the police if he does that again."

"Have you ever asked him why he hates Gerry so much?" Charlie asked.

"He says it's because of the jail sentence." Tara gives a bitter little laugh. "But the real reason is that he's a Chelsea fan."

"What?" This I can't believe.

Tara sighs as if she's tired of having to explain the obvious. "Fulham knocked Chelsea out of the FA Cup in 1976. And guess who scored the winning goal? Gerry Phelan."

"But that was years ago," says Charlie.

"To my dad, it's like yesterday. These things go deep, you know?"

"That's ridiculous," I protest. "It's only a game."

Charlie and Tara look at me, faintly shocked.

"Spoken like a true substitute," says Charlie quietly.

When I get home, it's to find there are two distinguished visitors sipping sherry with my parents in the sitting-room.

"Eve, you remember the Reverend Pardew and Mrs Fairbrother, don't you?" says my mother.

"Hi." I smile politely.

The Reverend Pardew, a weird-looking stick-insect of a man with tufts of hair sticking out from unexpected places on his face and scalp, stirs in his chair. "How was football, Eve?" he asks.

"Football? Oh, excellent, thanks."

"Actually, we've been discussing the question of your former manager."

There's something about the vicar's sincere, one-of-my-flock smile that I find almost threatening.

"He wasn't there today. He's banned."

"So we gather." He knits his hands together in a complicated way. "Your dad says that you and the girls are very keen that he should take you to the famous Area Finals."

"That's right." Suddenly I'm wishing that Lisa or Charlie were here to do the talking. "We wouldn't be there without him. If he's dropped as manager, we're not playing."

"Yes." Mrs Fairbrother, a big, tweedy woman who looks as if she should be out walking a couple of Labradors around her country estate, crosses her stout legs in a businesslike manner. "You see, there's a problem here, Eve," she says briskly. "This Mr Phelan may be a good manager but he's been less than honest, hasn't he?"

"That's in the past." I turn to Mrs Fairbrother. At least she talks to me in a direct way rather than in the creepy, patronizing tones of the vicar. "Why can't we just let bygones be bygones?"

"I'm not talking about his little spell in jail," she says. "He's paid his debt to society. But he should have been honest with you and with the school when he became manager."

It takes a couple of seconds for me to think of a reply to this new approach. "But he's been a manager before.

He ran his son Patrick's team two years ago. No one was worried about honesty then."

"That was different," says the Reverend Pardew.

"I don't see why."

"Because that was a boys' team – "

"And we're girls, right?" Suddenly my voice sounds tearful, almost shrieky. "It always comes down to the same thing."

"Eve, there's absolutely no call to be uncivil." My mother speaks up quickly, shooting an apologetic smile in the direction of the vicar.

"I understand your feelings," says Mrs Fairbrother. "But as governors, we have to take on board other issues, we have to look at the big picture. Have you heard about this girl Tara Williams?"

Once again, I feel myself wrong-footed. "Tara? What's she got to do with this?"

"Apparently she disappeared today. Bunked off school."

"Oh yeah, that." I shrug innocently. "I heard she's turned up now. Anyway what's it got to do with Mr Phelan?"

"The big picture." Mrs Fairbrother leans forward in her chair. "We have to take the interests of Broadhurst Comprehensive into account. Obviously your soccer games have been great fun but sometimes fun goes too far, gets out of hand. It can threaten the welfare of the whole school."

I try to interrupt but Mrs Fairbrother adds firmly, "Which is why we are one hundred per cent behind the headteacher in this matter."

91

I hold her eyes defiantly for a moment, then look away, defeated. "What's going to happen to Tara?"

"That's for Mr Morley to decide," says the vicar. "I imagine he'll take whatever disciplinary measure that is deemed appropriate."

For a moment there's silence in the sitting-room. Then the Reverend Pardew turns to my father as if I've just disappeared in a puff of smoke. "Now I believe there were other items we needed to discuss."

"Homework, Eve." My mother stands up and puts a hand on my shoulder. Shrugging her off, I leave the room without another word. As I climb the stairs, the sound of slightly embarrassed adult laughter follows me. They haven't heard the last of this.

Half an hour later, the two governors leave the house. My father trudges up the stairs, knocks on my door and, hearing my mumbled reply, comes in to stand behind me as I work at my desk.

"How's it going?"

"Fine."

"Eve, I tried."

I glance up and smile briefly. "Yeah, Dad. Thanks."

"Here." He hands me a battered old book he's holding. On the front cover is a photo of a couple of long-haired footballers battling over a ball. "I found this in a second-hand bookshop."

"*Score! Top Tips from the Stars of the Seventies,*" I read. "I don't think I'll be needing that somehow."

My father takes the book from me and opens it. There, on page 157, is a picture of a dark-haired, scruffy footballer, grinning at the camera. He had more hair in those days, and the face had the hope of youth, but the eyes are unmistakable. "SO HAPPY TOGETHER", read the headline. "FULHAM STAR REVEALS THE ART OF TEAMSMANSHIP."

After my father has left me, I push my English aside and settle down to read the wise words of the young Gerry Phelan.

There's no better feeling in the world than being in the centre of the park, the ball at your feet, the roar of the crowd in your ears. It's as if you're not an individual any more but are part of something bigger than you, something that, when it's working right, no group of mere men can defeat. It's called a team.

So you know exactly where George or Bobby or Steve will be without looking – you're all part of the same organism. This sense frees you to express yourself as you move across the pitch towards the goal. It's true freedom – we may each be different, with our own little quirks and problems, but together the team makes us strong.

With our own little quirks and problems. I put the book down and think about Tara. I've never met anyone with such a talent for self-destruction as that girl – the cliché "your own worst enemy" might have been invented for her. When things go wrong for Tara, her first reaction is to make them worse. If a teacher happens to give her a detention (and Tara's had more detentions than most of us have had school dinners), then she'll be burning on a short fuse all day. Within a couple of hours, she'll be in even bigger trouble, with detentions from here to next Christmas.

I think back to Mrs Fairbrother's words. Whatever disciplinary measure that is deemed appropriate. I have a bad feeling that it won't just be a detention this time.

Sighing, I return to *Score!*

A nd it's not just on the pitch. The manager, the coach, the groundstaff, the crowd – they're all part of that team. Lop off one limb from the body of the team and it's gone, finished, just a bunch of guys with a leather ball. Even if you're injured or suspended you've got to be part of it until you're back. It's where our strength comes from as individuals – the freedom provided by friendship and looking after one another.

That settles it. I need to talk to Tara, to see if she's all right. I walk to the upstairs telephone and dial her number.

"Hello, Eve." Mrs Williams seems strangely subdued. There's none of the background din that I expect when I telephone Tara.

Distantly I hear the growling tones of Mr Williams near by.

"Tara can't come to the phone right now." It's probably my imagination but Tara's mum sounds scared. "Can she ring you back?"

"Yes, please. Tonight, if possible."

It's another two hours before I hear from Tara. She

sounds tired. Her dad has gone to the pub but she can't speak for long, she tells me.

"Was he all right tonight, your dad?"

"Yeah, not too bad. He's happy now."

"Happy?"

"He's got what he wanted. I've been banned from playing the Area Finals. Mr Morley and he agreed this evening." A note of fake cheerfulness has entered Tara's voice. "They decided that it was time for me to lose something I really cared about. And what was the only thing I really care about? Bingo."

"Oh Tara, that's terrible."

"Shut up terrible. It means you're in the team for a start."

"I don't *want* to be in the team. I like being substitute. Anyway, even if we do play in the Finals, which I doubt, we can't go in with a squad of five."

"You know what you have to do, then." Tara's mumbling now, as if reluctant to continue talking.

"Tara. What are you talking about? What can we do?"

"Get the Yank," she snaps. "She'd go for it like a shot."

"The Yank? Stevie? But you hate her."

"Yeah, but she can play football. If she helps get the Hotshots through to the Final, that's all that matters. I'll be back for that."

"Are you serious, Tara?" To tell the truth, I've never seen Tara as someone with team spirit. "I mean, even if we do play Stevie in the team, who goes in goal?"

"Roberta. I phoned Gerry and discussed it." Tara seems to have taken her mouth away from the telephone.

"You phoned Gerry? I don't believe it."

"And why not? I'm not totally selfish even if everybody thinks so."

"I didn't say you were selfish," I explain patiently. "It's just that you're not normally this organized."

"Put it down to shock. You reckon Roberta would do it?"

"I'm not sure – in fact I'm not sure about the whole thing."

"Shut up you're not sure. You can win the Area Finals – win 'em for Tara. When are the governors talking to Morley about Gerry?"

"They're not." I explain what happened at the meeting that night.

For a moment, Tara's silent. Then she says, "They're not going to beat us, no way."

"'Course not." I hear a door slamming down the phone.

"Gotta run."

And Tara hangs up on me.

CHAPTER SIX

A Dork Too Far

"**Y**o."

The unmistakable, booming voice of Stevie Rostand echoes through the park as she arrives five minutes late for our final practice the Saturday morning before the Area Finals of the Met. She swings her purple and gold bag and throws it in an arc towards where we're sitting. It lands a few inches from Lisa who glances up irritably.

"Yo, Hotshots." Stevie tries again.

"Hi," mutters Ellie unenthusiastically. The rest of us continue getting ready for the practice in silence.

The fact is, Stevie's addition to the team may have helped us out of a spot but it's done nothing for morale. Humming loudly to herself, she pulls a pair of trainers out of her bag. They're so high-tech they look as if they've been made for a space walk or something.

Stevie's just too confident for her own good. When we asked her to join the team, she behaved as if she had been expecting to be asked all along. Even now, a week later and a few days before the Area Finals, she turns up late for practice. Whenever she's playing, she mutters to herself as if she were in her own private little world.

"Didn't see any of you down at the boys' final last night," she says. "The guys asked me where you were."

"What have the *guys* ever done for us?" Roberta asks sourly.

This was another thing. In spite of being a Hotshot, Stevie has insisted on remaining friends with Jason.

"I hear they lost," says Lisa with undisguised satisfaction.

"Yeah, bummer." Stevie stands up, jogs on the spot and does some stretching exercises. "Jase scored a neat goal, though."

"Four one." Lisa smiles at the rest of us. "Doesn't sound too neat to me."

"Hey, you dorks, get real." Stevie shows a flash of anger at last. "They're not the enemy, you know. Have you any idea how petty and small-minded all this bitching makes you seem?"

Before we can reply, Patrick, who's standing near by, tells us to pick teams. Without any great enthusiasm, we move into the old routine.

It was Gerry's idea that we should continue practising even though we're still determined not to appear for Area Finals if our manager is banned. Patrick wants to be a sports instructor, Gerry told us. He needs the practice. Anyway, it's still possible that the headteacher will change his mind.

So, reluctantly, we practise.

But these days it's not the same. There's a tetchy, unreal atmosphere to what we're doing. Ever since she was banned, Tara has stayed away and, without her shouting and joking from the goal line, we play in an unnatural silence, interrupted only by the occasional mutterings from Stevie.

Patrick does his best but, behind the hunky good looks, he's just a shy fifteen-year-old with a talent for football. He lets the niggling remarks, the sarcastic backchat, go unchecked. Good on tactics, weak on morale – that's Patrick.

That morning, it occurs to me that the Hotshots' greatest strength, our teamwork, is unravelling before our eyes. Stevie, for example, is good – a strong player – but she seems to have elected herself the team's new super ego. This, of course, is traditionally Lisa's role. No wonder that, after a couple of practices, they've ceased to pass to one another or even acknowledge the other's existence on the pitch.

Halfway through the practice game, I notice that Stevie's darting looks in the direction of the playground near by. Then I see what has attracted her attention.

Two familiar figures are ambling towards the swings as if they have just happened to be taking a walk in the park. Jason and Dominic. With typical generosity of spirit, the two boys have decided to try and disrupt our last practice.

For a while, we manage to ignore them as they sit on the swings, talking loudly, chuckling every time one of us makes a mistake. After about five minutes, Patrick wanders over to speak to them but Jason's ready for him. I hear the words, "Public park, ennit?" Defeated, Patrick shrugs and turns back to us.

For some reason, our game seems to attract more attention than usual that day. People walking their dogs pause to watch us heaving and panting in the morning sun. A tall, crop-headed man in tracksuit and trainers stands near by, before wandering over to us as we take a five-minute break.

"Broadhurst Girls, is it?" he asks Patrick.

"Yeah. Hotshots."

"They've got a tough game next week," says the stranger casually.

We look at him with more interest.

Patrick asks how he knows about the Area Finals.

"I take an interest in youth football." The man looks away, as if he's already said too much. "I've seen a few games with the Sulgrave Girls. They're your opposition on Tuesday."

"What are they like?" asks Lisa, voicing the question the rest of us hadn't dared ask.

"Pretty useful." The stranger nods slowly. "Unbeaten this year, I'm told. A couple of their girls would be scouted by one of the big professional clubs if they were boys."

We look at one another gloomily. Ask a silly question.

"You'll be all right so long as your defence is good. They've scored over fifty goals in the league this year," the stranger continues.

"League?" Roberta, who has never exactly been happy about replacing Tara in goal, speaks up nervously. "They play in a league?"

"'Course. Don't you? They won the local league and the cup last year. Now they're going for a treble with the Met." The man glances at his watch, then winks at Patrick in an irritating man-to-man way. "Good luck on Tuesday." Whistling softly to himself, he walks off across the park.

When we resume playing, it's with even less conviction than before. The sun is growing hotter by the minute. If we play at all next Tuesday, it will be against a team of superwomen. Jason and Dominic are lolling on the sidelines, jeering whenever we make a mistake.

It's Stevie who goes too far. Ellie has just taken the ball down the left wing, centring it to where Lisa stands, with Stevie making a run to her right. Under normal circumstances, Lisa would control the ball, draw Charlie in defence, before releasing it to her fellow striker to score. Instead she blasts it over Roberta in goal.

"Jesus, Lisa!" This time it was more than a mutter from Stevie.

"Eh?" Lisa whirls towards her.

"I was like totally unmarked," goes Stevie. She turns towards the boys, who're now rolling around on the grass, helpless with laughter, and spreads her hands in a what-can-you-do gesture.

As Tara might say, she's now gone ridiculously beyond.

Lisa storms up to her and pushes her hard in the back.

"Either you're with us or you're with them," she

screams. "If you really want to play with those losers, why don't you – " She managed an impressive stream of swearwords.

"You just butt out, you dork," Stevie yells and grabs her by the shirt.

For a moment, it looks as though there's going to be a full-scale fight on the pitch but Patrick hurries over to separate the two girls. The colour has drained from Stevie's face. "You need help, you know," she hisses at Lisa. "What are you, some kind of psycho?"

Lisa looks away tearfully.

"Right." Patrick sighs and looks at his watch. "We'll leave the practice there for this morning, all right?"

There's silence among the Hotshots as Lisa and Stevie continue to eyeball one another.

"If any of you want to leave this team" – Patrick raises his voice – "you can ring my father. Otherwise I'll assume that the Hotshots are still together for the Area Finals on Tuesday."

I glance over to where the boys were sitting but they've gone – satisfied, no doubt, by their morning's work.

Discussing the Hotshots with my parents is like trying to explain cricket to a couple of Eskimos – they aren't that interested and, even if they were, they wouldn't exactly understand how it works. But, after that last disastrous practice, there's no alternative. I need advice and my parents are the only adults I can turn to.

Yet somehow, as we sit in our front room, the story

comes out all wrong. The great heroic tale of loyalty against self-interest, team spirit against personal greed, the great quest for glory, doesn't sound like that when I tell it to Mum and Dad. A drunken loser of a manager. A goalkeeper banned for ill-discipline. Boys jeering from the sidelines. Girls on the point of tearing one another's hair out. So much for the Beautiful Game.

"I see." My father purses his lips thoughtfully as I finish my account. From the way he glances at Mum, it's obvious that all his fears about my becoming involved in the Hotshots have been confirmed. "So it's a question of pulling out of the contest, and proving everyone right or compromising your principles about Gerry Phelan?"

"Yeah." I stare hard at him, daring him to smile.

"You're caught on the horns of a dilemma."

"Heads you lose, tails they win," Mum chimes in unhelpfully.

"We need to analyse when it all first began to go wrong," says my father in the tone of voice he adopts when he's helping me with maths homework.

"It was when Gerry Phelan was barred by Mr Morley."

"And there's absolutely no possibility of his changing his mind, I'm afraid." My father smiles, almost embarrassed. "After I drew a blank with the governors, I put a call through to him. He seems to think this is a test of his authority."

"Great," I mutter.

"You need to make him think that reinstating Gerry Phelan is his idea," says Mum suddenly. "If you could just present a united front to him – don't bully or threaten, merely point out that the Hotshots have been victims of male prejudice. That way, he'll be able to take the credit for your success – "

"But we've done that, haven't we?" I sigh moodily. It was probably crazy to think my parents could help.

"Does he actually have to be manager?" asks Mum.

I'm about to interrupt with a sarcastic remark about making him Chairman of the Hotshots or something, when I'm struck by a sudden flash of inspiration. "Kit!" I say, leaping to my feet.

Mum and Dad look at me as if I've gone crazy.

"When we played last time, Gerry provided the kit."

"Kit manager." My mother smiles. "Very important job, that."

"But you'll have to get your Mr Phelan to agree," says my father. "And the team had better stop squabbling. You need a united front to persuade Mr Morley."

"Right." My mind is racing.

"Who would have thought we'd be sitting here, solemnly discussing football?" Mum gets to her feet. "What about your ballet exam next month?"

"I'll be able to concentrate on that after the big game," I laugh. "At the moment my feet are confused – they want to go up on points when I'm playing football and clump about when I'm meant to be doing *pas de deux*."

"You were always so keen on – "

"All *right*, Mum," I interrupt. "I'll practise tonight. But this afternoon I've got to see Gerry."

"You're not going round there by yourself," says my mother firmly.

For a moment, I consider which of the Hotshots I should take. The only one I trust completely not to say the wrong thing is Charlie and I know she's going to a football match with her mum today.

I smile at my father ingratiatingly. "Were you doing anything this afternoon?" I ask. "You won't have to see Gerry. Just drive me round there. Please."

Dad looks doubtful. "Football," he sighs.

"Pretty please."

An hour later, I'm at Gerry's flat while my father waits downstairs. I glance out of the window and see him, tapping the steering-wheel nervously like a man in a getaway car.

"I mustn't be long," I tell Gerry. "My dad wouldn't let me walk round here alone."

Gerry's sitting in an armchair like someone who last moved from there several weeks ago. "You should have asked him in," he says.

"No. I needed to see you alone."

"Well, I haven't got much time either." He glances at me as if to check whether I react to this remark. "There's a film on TV."

I sit down nervously on the chair opposite Gerry. "We need your help, Mr Phelan," I say quietly. I go on to explain what has been going wrong with our practices – how Patrick has been doing his best, how the team without Tara and with Stevie has been falling apart. It's quite a little speech. By the time I've finished, Gerry is staring into space, deep in thought. "Too many egos." I laugh nervously. "And Stevie Rostand is even worse than Lisa. You'd think she'd be grateful for the chance to play with us."

As I taper off feebly, Gerry reaches for a packet of cigarettes that lies on the arm of his chair. "When I first came over from Ireland, I was just like that," he says distantly. He lights up and the smoke from his cigarette catches the sunlight shining through his grimy window. "On the pitch, off the pitch, I was the real kiddo. Me, me, me. Look after Number One. Didn't matter who won the game, so long as I proved how great I was." He smiles at the memory.

"Really," I say, thinking to myself that this isn't exactly the perfect moment for nostalgic reminiscences.

"You know why? Because I was frightened. I was alone. No confidence. No sense of belonging. Your little American's like that."

"But she's rich," I protest. "She's good looking. She behaves as if she's so superior to everyone."

"I'll bet you she's scared. Like Lisa. Like Tara. Like you. We've all got our own demons that we're hiding from." He hesitates. "The good team is one that unites the demons and turns them against the opposition."

"I suppose Stevie did stick up for Tara when she was in trouble with the police at the fairground."

"It's the same with all of you," Gerry continues. "By herself, Lisa Martin's a little prima donna, her mother in miniature. Tara's a crazy tearaway. Charlie, Roberta,

Ellie – they all have their weaknesses. Stevie's a spoilt brat. You're afraid of being a mummy's girl, a nervous little only child" – ignoring my attempt to interrupt, Gerry raises his voice – "but together you're strong. You're no longer individuals with your own weird little problems. You're Hotshots. United."

He shrugs and looks away, as if suddenly embarrassed. "End of sermon," he mutters.

"The problem is that we're not united unless we have the right manager."

Gerry glances at me irritably. "We've been through all that," he says. "I've done what I can do."

"I was wondering – " Taking a deep breath, I explain my plan about appointing him kit manager. Except, for some reason, I tell him that the whole thing was Tara's idea.

"Kit manager?" There's a flash of anger in his grey eyes. "You want Gerry Phelan to be kit manager?"

"Only to get you past Mr Morley."

"Smuggle me in through the back door, is it?" He shakes his head. "My girl, there is a limit and you've overstepped it."

It's time for the last throw of the dice. I stand up and pull a piece of paper from my back pocket. "'Lop off one limb from the body of the team and it's gone, finished, just a bunch of guys with a leather ball,'" I read out. "'Even if you're injured or suspended you've got to be part of it until you're back. That's where our strength comes from as individuals – the freedom provided by friendship and looking after one another.'"

Gerry says nothing.

"You know who wrote that, Mr Phelan?"

"Some bloody – " There's a crack in his voice as if suddenly the words are having to be forced out. "Some bloody cock-eyed optimist from a bygone age."

For a moment there's silence in the room. "Maybe what you said about us all having our demons goes for managers as well as players," I say quietly.

At last Mr Phelan raises his eyes to me. He's smiling. "If the whole team support this plan, I'll go along with it."

"Thanks, Mr Phelan." It's almost a shout of relief. He shrinks back in his chair as if I'm about to hug him or something. "Where can we find you tonight?"

"You can't. I'm at the Latimer Working Men's Club."

"We'll be there." I walk quickly to the door.

"But they don't allow – "

"See you, Gerry."

And I'm gone.

"Hi, Lisa, it's Eve."

"Hi."

"Guess what? Stevies' just rang me to say she's really sorry about this morning. She was just upset by Jason and Dominic."

"Oh yeah, I really believe that."

"It's true. And Tara's got this plan to sort things out and get Mr Phelan back."

"Plan?"

"And it might just work. What are you doing this evening, Lisa . . . ?"

"Hi Stevie, it's Eve."

"Yo."

"Look, Lisa's just been on the phone saying how sorry she was about what happened in the park."

"Yeah?"

"She really admires you. She wants to be friends."

"Friends?" Stevie laughs. "In her dreams."

"She told me that she feels terrible about what she did – particularly because she admires your football."

There's a stunned silence from the other end of the phone. "Eve, are you putting me on?" Stevie asks uncertainly.

"No, I'm not. Anyway, Tara's come up with this plan which requires all our help."

"Lisa admires my football?"

"We all do, Stevie. We think you're just great. Now about this evening . . ."

"Hi, Tara."

"Hey, Evie."

"You heard about the practice."

"Ellie rang me. Exit Hotshots, right?"

"Not if you're prepared to help. I've rung the others and we're going to meet up tonight."

"Tonight? What for?"

"Well, you've worked out this plan, see."

"Shut up I've worked out a plan."

"No, listen. People pay more attention to you than they do to me. Don't ask me why but it's a fact."

"Maybe it's because they know I'll thump them if they don't."

"Maybe. Now, I've done all the groundwork. All you've got to do is pretend that it was your idea for Gerry to be our kit manager."

"Kit manager? *Lame*."

"Yeah, yeah, Tara. Just shut up – "

"Shut up shut up – "

"Just listen to what we're going to do, will you?"

I've walked past the Latimer Working Men's Club on my way to school every day but I never thought that I would be visiting it one Saturday night as part of a delegation of seven footballers. In fact, I always assumed that the club was nothing but a big derelict house these days – not only does it look as if the building is about to fall down, but the whole idea of a Working Men's Club seems to belong to a bygone age. I mean, where are the working men these days? Even if they've got a job, they don't exactly go around calling themselves "working men".

But I'm wrong. It's just past eight o'clock as we nervously approach the front door. As we open the glass doors into the reception area, we're almost knocked back out into the street by the volume of music and raised voices coming from the club itself.

"Yes?" An elderly man with a complexion like raspberry ripple looks up at us from a desk. His face is a picture of undisguised hostility.

It's been agreed that Lisa, who's good at the whole charm thing, will do the talking.

"We're here to see Mr Gerry Phelan," she says sweetly.

A mumbling sound emanates from the old man's throat.

"I beg your pardon?" says Lisa.

"No kids." The man looks away. "No kids in the club."

"It's extremely urgent," says Lisa patiently. "And it will only take five minutes." She gives the old man the benefit of her million-dollar smile. "Perhaps he could come out here to see us?"

Muttering to himself, the man struggles to his feet.

"Just tell him the Hotshots are here," Lisa calls after him.

Still grumbling, the man pushes a swing door behind him, briefly revealing a large, smoke-filled room, full of men and women dressed in their Saturday best. On a stage at the back of the room, some sort of band is playing with a lot more volume than tune.

"Oh, wow." Stevie recoils visibly.

"Welcome to the real England," smiles Ellie.

To our dismay, the old man returns a few moments later, alone. He stands at the swing door, looking at us with deep disgust, before jerking his head in the direction of the room. Then he shuffles back into the dance-room, leaving the door to swing in our faces.

"I think he wants us to follow him," Roberta says nervously.

"Charming," mutters Lisa.

The band doesn't actually stop playing as we make our entrance, but there seems to be a brief, stunned pause, as if even the musicians are amazed by what they're seeing. Children at the club! On a Saturday night!

As the drinkers at the nearby tables peer at us through the smoke, Stevie moves closer to me as if she has been asked to walk into a den of blood-crazed English child-murderers. Sensing another attack of the oh-wows, I take her arm, murmuring quietly, "Do not say one word."

Gerry's at a corner table with two other men. The empty beer glasses on the table and high colour on the men's faces suggest that they've been at the club for a good part of the evening.

"Well, well. The Hotshots." Gerry Phelan's smile, directed at me, lacks its usual warmth. "What a surprise."

"We need to talk, Mr Phelan," says Lisa. "We want your help. All of us."

"Help." Gerry takes a long swig of beer. "Just play football is all you need to do."

"It's going wrong." Ellie steps forward. "We thought playing in the Met would just be a question of playing in matches and winning but it all seems to have got complicated. And the problems have got nothing to do with football at all."

Gerry gives us a long, drunken look. "That does tend to be the way of things," he says slowly.

He stands up, patting one of his friends on the

shoulder, then beckons us to follow him. As we cross the room once more, winding our way single file between the tables, jokey comments reach us through the smoke.

"It's the Pied Piper of Tipperary," says one man.

"He'll be after buying them all a Guinness," laughs another.

Ignoring them, Mr Phelan opens the door to a smaller room, in the centre of which is a long shiny table. He slumps down on to one of the chairs. "Make yourselves at home, Hotshots," he says, waving in the direction of the other chairs. We sit down and, between us, explain our problem – the head, how the boys have gone out of their way to disrupt practice, the disagreements between the players.

"Patrick's great." This is Lisa, of course. "But we need you back as manager."

"Or kit manager." Gerry smiles at me.

"It's just a title." Tara speaks up at last. "Eve thought – or rather I thought – that Mr Morley would agree to that."

Gerry sits deep in thought. "All right," he says finally. "But only if the head agrees."

"Yeah." There's relief among the Hotshots. Stevie gives a little whoop of joy.

"At least we'll have a chance now," says Roberta. "We'll still probably get beaten but at least we'll put up a fight."

"What you talking about?" Gerry frowns.

Roberta tells him about the stranger in the park, about his inside information on Sulgrave Girls.

As she finishes her story, we're amazed to see that he's chuckling to himself as if he has just heard a hilarious joke.

"It's not *that* funny," I say coldly.

"The oldest trick in the book," says Mr Phelan eventually. "It's called psyching the other team out. You get them so nervous that they think they've lost before they've even left home."

"You mean he did it on purpose?" Roberta asks. "He was on their side?"

"Probably their manager." Gerry stands up. "Now was that all, girls?"

"Thank you, Mr Phelan," I say softly.

Gerry gives me a conspiratorial wink. "You're very welcome, Eve."

There are muted celebrations as we emerge from the smoke and noise of the club on to the street outside.

"Phase one completed," smiles Ellie.

I clap Lisa on the back. "You were brilliant," I say.

"Shucks, it was nothing."

"Good plan, Tara," goes Roberta.

Tara shrugs modestly.

"You know, I think we can win on Tuesday," says Roberta, as if the thought has only just occurred to her.

Stevie is waving the air in front of her as if trying to rid herself of the smell of the club. "If we all don't die of passive smoking first. Was that old soak really your manager?"

We turn to her and for a moment there's trouble in the air once more.

"Hey, cool it." Stevie holds up her hands in mock surrender. "It was a joke, guys."

One of the lessons I've learnt during this Hotshots summer is that the best way to get things done is not to scream and shout – the Tara method, you could call it – but cunningly to engineer events so that the person in authority thinks that it was him who made the decision. This is particularly true of headteachers.

"Kit?"

At lunchtime on Monday Lisa, Ellie and I put the last phase of our plan into effect. Mr Morley has smiled patiently as we ask yet again whether Mr Phelan could manage us for the Area Finals of the Met.

Unfortunately, Mr Phelan has been proved not to be a suitable supervisor for children, he tells us wearily.

He smiles patiently as Lisa informs him that, if he wants the Broadhurst Hotshots to win, it's essential that Mr Phelan is there to advise us.

It would be unfortunate if we lost, of course, but the great thing is to have taken part.

"I honestly wish I could help you, girls." Mr Morley sighs. "But there's an important principle at stake here. I've made my decision and there's no way that I can go back on it."

So we play our last, final throw. I mention the kit.

"How d'you mean you have no kit?" he asks.

"It was Mr Phelan who provided the kit for us in the first round," I say. "But if he's not there . . ."

"But there's the school kit."

"Each of the boys took their shirts home after their match," says Lisa. "Even if they bring them in tomorrow, they'll be all dirty and smelly."

"Those purple shirts that we wore last time are lucky for us," says Ellie.

"Yes," I say carefully. "It was just luck that, for the first round, Mr Phelan was both our coach and our kit manager."

"Kit manager?" The headteacher frowns, deep in thought. I swear it must take a good twenty seconds for the penny to drop. Suddenly he can see it – a way round the problem which won't involve him losing face or backing down. "What would you say if – just thinking on my feet here – if Mr Phelan were invited to come along to the Area Finals as kit manager?"

We gasp with surprise at this amazing, inspired suggestion that of course would never have occurred to us in a million trillion years.

"I think that would be very, *very* possible, sir," says Lisa.

"So, you mean, he still wouldn't be manager but he would be involved with the team as kit manager." I put on my most creepy, admiring voice.

"I know nothing about this officially, you understand," the headteacher says quickly.

"Of course not, sir," I smile. "It's all unofficial."

We leave Mr Morley, sitting at his desk, tapping his fingers on the blotter before him. He wears the expression of a man who realizes he has just been out-manoeuvred but can't work out quite how it happened.

CHAPTER SEVEN

The True Story

The day of the Area Finals, I wake at dawn, my mind seething with unanswered questions.

To judge by his slurred speech at the Latimer, Gerry Phelan seems to be drinking again. Will he be sober for the big game? Will he turn up at all?

And what about Patrick? The last time Lisa played in a serious game in front of her beloved she was, to use Mr Phelan's phrase, as much use as a one-legged man in a bottom-kicking competition. Will True Love bloom just when it's least needed?

Then there's the private competition between Lisa and Stevie for Prima Donna of the Year. What chance is there – I turn restlessly in my bed – that they'll put the Hotshots before their private rivalry?

What happens if someone gets injured and I have to go on as substitute? I curl up in bed, trying not to think of it.

But I hear the murmurs of amusement as I take to the pitch, skinny legs and all. I fall over the ball. The crowd rocks with laughter. Opposition players ghost past me as if I'm not there. The other Hotshots are screaming at me now –

"Eve!"

OK – my right leg kicks desperately at the blankets – I'm doing my best –

"*Eve!* Breakfast!"

I pull the sheets over my head. The day I've been waiting for is here. I wish it would just go away.

When I reach school, there's a general sense of anticipation in the air. As I make my way through the playground to hang up my coat, a group of boys, including Jason, is hanging around outside the entrance to the classroom.

"Ready for the big game, supersub?" Jason calls out.

"Yeah, but no thanks to you," I mutter, brushing past him.

"Oooh, pressure. Can't take the pressure," he jeers in a childish voice which doesn't quite conceal his envy.

Even Mr Morley seems to be caught up in the general mood, as if at this late stage he has suddenly discovered the joys of competition.

"Today, as we all know, is the day of the Hotshots," he announces to the entire school at Assembly. "It has been a remarkable achievement to have reached the Area Finals of the Metropolitan Cup. This means – " he beams around the hall proudly – "that Broadhurst Comprehensive has one of the two best Under 13 girls' teams in this entire region."

"He's changed his tune," murmurs Roberta, sitting in the row behind me.

Ellie, to my left, nudges me. "I feel strange," she says.

"For this I'm sure the girls would join me in a debt of gratitude to Miss Wilson, who started the ball rolling, to coin a phrase, until her unfortunate injury, and to Patrick Phelan for helping out with some of the coaching. Then there's Mr Armstrong who made sure that the school van was available."

"Eh?" What the rest of us are thinking to ourselves, Tara — who else? — has to express out loud.

"*Eh?*"

Briefly, Mr Morley's eyes rest on her.

"Other people were involved, of course," he continues carefully. "Too many to mention. I simply want to wish the Broadhurst Girls' Team — the, er, Hotshots — our best wishes for this evening's game. I'm sure that the spirit with which you'll play will reflect the important lessons about companionship, care, endeavour which, in this school, we have all learnt to cherish. You'll remember the lines I like to quote: 'Keep your eyes wide open, the chance won't come again.' Well I'm sure that on today of all days . . ."

As the headteacher moves effortlessly into the usual, well-meaning blather, Ellie nudges me again.

"I feel sick," she says.

"Yeah, me too. Typical Morley," I whisper. "*Now* he talks about working together."

"No. I mean, really. I'm going to throw up."

I glance across at Ellie. Her face has turned a delicate shade of green. Suddenly she stands up and pushes past me, making hurriedly for the door.

119

It takes a moment for the terrible truth to dawn on me. Ellie's ill. With anyone else, it might have been nerves, but she's never been the type to spew up out of sheer terror.

As soon as Assembly is over, Lisa, Tara and I sprint to the girls' lavatory. From one of the cubicles, there's the unmistakable sound of someone bringing up their breakfast.

"Ellie!" Lisa calls out. "Are you all right?"

"What do *you* think?" Ellie moans.

"I don't believe this," mutters Lisa. "On this of all days."

"Yo, y'all." Stevie breezes in, presumably to examine her latest bright orange tracksuit in the mirror. She pauses when she sees our gloomy faces. "Something wrong?"

As if in reply, Ellie makes some more disgusting guttural noises from her cubicle.

"Oh, gross," says Stevie, checking herself in a nearby mirror. "Who's the barf queen?"

"Ellie," says Tara.

"Sheesh, poor old Ellie." She's about to leave when the full significance of the situation dawns on her. "*What*? If Ellie's too ill to play, we'll have to use – " She turns to me.

"Thank you very much, Stevie," I say coldly. "I'm really touched by your confidence."

It seems that, for a lot of people, an evening spent watching five-a-side football in a police training park outside London is a perfect summer's entertainment.

Within minutes of our arrival at Dartmouth Park in the school van, it's clear that we have friends and enemies among the crowd gathered there.

"Talk about a major police presence," says Tara, looking around her. Half of the cars parked near by seem to have blue lights on their roofs. Constables in shirtsleeves stand behind tables on which pamphlets explaining the wonderful work of the police force are displayed.

In the centre of the park are two pitches, surrounded by hardboard walls, over which spectators can view the game taking place inside.

"It's like a bullfight," I say to Lisa as we approach one of the pitches.

"Yeah, and we're the bull they've all come to see slaughtered." Lisa doesn't seem to be in one of her more positive moods.

For a moment we watch a game between older girls which is already being played.

"They're enormous," Lisa murmurs. "If Sulgrave Girls look anything like that, we might as well go home."

We wander back to the van, where Ellie is sitting palely in the front seat. She has spent the day at home, being fed soup and vitamins by her mother, with the result that by now the green has faded from her cheeks to be replaced by a ghostly white.

Under pressure from all of us, she has agreed at least to start the game in the hope that the roar of the crowd and the prospect of Cup glory will make her forget her tormented stomach.

Gathered uncertainly around the van are a group of the Broadhurst supporters – Lisa's mum, standing with a little man in a silver shell-suit, Charlie's mother and father and, of course, my parents, who have never been late for anything in their lives.

As we stand, looking around for Mr Phelan and Patrick, a large car arrives, bearing all of Tara's family, give or take a baby or two.

"They think I'll be playing," Tara mutters. "My father's convinced that Mr Morley's going to change his mind about my suspension at the last minute."

Mr Williams gets out of the car and strides towards us like a boxer on his way into the ring before a title fight. He's a big, broad man and, like his daughter, he's much given to expressing his opinions at the worst possible moment.

"Warmed up, are we?" he booms.

"The game's not for another hour, Dad," says Tara. "We're waiting for the kit manager."

Luckily Mr Williams fails to pick up on this careless remark. "Now where's that headteacher?" he says. "I want a word with him about – "

"Dad, no," Tara interrupts.

There's a burst of cheering from a nearby ring as one of the teams scores and, for a moment, our little group watches in silence. An expression of pained tolerance seems to have settled on my father's face. Being jostled by a crowd of footballing parents in a police park on a balmy summer's evening when he could be reading the *Guardian* on the patio as Mum prepares dinner is not exactly his idea of a good time.

To tell the truth, I feel slightly removed from the general excitement. Training in the playground, playing in the park, seems a million miles away from the tension of tonight.

"D'you remember Mr Phelan's words at our first practice?" I ask Charlie who's standing next to me. "He asked us if we were there to play football or just have a bit of fun." I sigh. "Suddenly, I think I prefer fun."

"Too late now, girl."

"Come on, you Hotshots!" From across the park come the unmistakable sounds of young Neanderthals on the loose. Jason and five of his disciples amble towards us, having taken the long bus ride out of town to Dartmouth Park – presumably for the pleasure of seeing us lose.

"Get lost, you guys," says Stevie uneasily.

"What's the matter?" asks Dominic. "Don't you want our support?"

By now the boys have attracted Mr Williams' unfriendly attention. Grumbling, and with a few more muted chants and grunts, they move off in the direction of a nearby hot dog stand.

Someone taps me on the shoulder. I turn to see Jamie O'Keeffe.

"Yo, Eve," he says quietly.

"Jamie!" Lisa laughs. "For a moment, I thought we were going to be without our mascot. How did you get here?"

"Got a lift," says Jamie, adding quietly, "your kit manager is in the car park."

"Our kit manager!" Lisa bursts out.

Jamie puts a finger to his lips. "He wants to see you away from the parents."

Casually we turn to our group of supporters. "We're just off to get changed now," said Roberta.

"What about the kit?" Charlie's father asks.

"It's been delivered to the changing-rooms," I say quickly.

As Ellie steps queasily out of her parents' car to join us, Lisa's mother totters forward on her high heels, a trail of expensive perfume in her wake. She gives Lisa an extravagant hug. "Break a leg, darling," she trills.

"Shut up break a leg," Tara mutters. "That's not very nice."

"It's a showbiz greeting," Lisa explains, extricating herself from her mother's arms. "It means good luck."

Suddenly it's as if we're going off to a war or something, with parents wishing us luck as we move away.

"How are you feeling?" I ask Ellie as we follow Jamie towards the clubhouse.

"Nervous," says Ellie. "But I'll be all right for the game."

I sigh with genuine relief. A couple of minutes on the pitch at the end of the game will do me just fine. Anything more is likely to be a disaster.

Gerry Phelan sits on the hood of his car, dressed in a dark blue suit, tie and – a typical Gerry touch – a pair of brand new white trainers. As we approach, I'm relieved to see that his face is pale and alert, with none of those tell-tale red blotches around the cheeks.

"Evening," he says briskly, pushing himself off the bonnet. He picks up the kit bag and passes it to Lisa.

"Yeah!" She smiles as she holds up the bag. "Our lucky kit."

"Lucky?" The manager frowns. "You won't be needing luck today. You're going to win."

It's strange – even before Gerry has given us his team talk, each of us feels calmer, more confident. He's got that quiet authority you find in just a few adults, that ability to make you believe that together you can make it work.

So, as Gerry begins to talk, our anxieties seem to lift. I look around me and I see that each of us, perhaps for the first time, feels like a winner. Yes, even me.

"Now, Ellie – " Gerry places a hand on her shoulder. "Are you well enough to play?"

The colour seems to be returning to Ellie's cheeks now.

She nods. "I feel a bit weak but I think I'll be OK."

"You're on. Don't try to save yourself in the first part of the game. Play it minute by minute. If you feel ill, just give me a sign – I'll be watching out for you. Remember, if you come off, we have a useful substitute."

Substitute? I look around me.

"That's you, Eve," says Gerry with that private smile he seems to reserve for me. "Remember it was you who scored the goal that got us here."

I grow about six inches at this point.

"Now, Stevie." Gerry turns to the American. "My son tells me you have a useful left peg."

"Peg? Excuse me?"

"Foot. You'll play down the left with Ellie on the right of midfield. Charlie's in defence with the captain as striker."

I glance at Stevie expecting her to make some sort of comment about her being the best striker, but no – she actually smiles at Lisa. Phew.

With quiet precision, Gerry explains how we should approach the game. Once we emerge from the changing-room, it's going to be a match like any other, he tells us. There will be noise. There will be cheers and groans. There will be anxious parents. But only one thing matters – the team and the game of football. It's essential to start calmly, pass the ball around – chances in front of goal will come later. The most important thing to remember is to be firm in defence in those jittery first two minutes.

Gerry has just explained that penalties should be taken by Lisa, free kicks by Stevie, when there's a sort of bull-like roar behind us.

Emerging from around the clubhouse is Tara's dad, Mr Williams.

"I warned you!" he yells as he marches towards us. He shakes a fist in Gerry's direction, his face contorted with rage. "You're not fit to be a manager. You were banned by the head. I'm not standing by having these girls managed by a Paddy ex-convict."

"I believe my title is kit manager," says Gerry Phelan evenly as Mr Williams brushes past us towards him.

"And what you doing now? Explaining to them how to tie their bootlaces? Once a conman, always a conman – that's what I always say."

"Dad!"

Tara steps forward quickly and stands between the two men. She once told me that her father was the only person she had ever been afraid of, but there's no sign of fear now.

"This is nothing to do with you, Dad," she says firmly. "Mr Morley has cleared Gerry Phelan as kit manager – "

"Get out of the way, Tara."

"Anyway," Tara continues. "I'm not in the team so it's none of our business, is it?"

Mr Williams' right arm seems to twitch as if his natural reflex is to lash out, but Tara stands her ground.

"He's a bloody jailbird, girl," goes Mr Williams, almost pleading.

"Yeah." Tara stares her father in the eye with a coolness I never knew she possessed. "Well, he's not the only person to have been in trouble with the police, is he?"

"I'll – " Mr Williams is backing away now. "I'll sort you out – " he stabs a fat finger in Tara's direction – "back home." He turns and bustles away angrily.

Tara closes her eyes and takes a deep breath.

"Well done, Tara," says Gerry, putting an arm around her shoulder. "That was brave."

"Stupid more like," Tara manages to say, her voice cracking as if she's about to cry.

Gerry Phelan smiles and turns to the rest of us. "The Hotshots spirit," he says, as if nothing has happened. "Tara's just shown us what can be done with a bit of courage and determination. Now you lot go and do it on the pitch."

By the time we emerge from the changing-rooms some fifteen minutes later, the crowd around the pitches seems to have swelled to a couple of hundred people. As Gerry leads us to a practice area in the corner of the park, a strange emptiness – like I feel before music exams only much worse – fills my stomach.

Beyond the pitches I can see some girls in blue shirts warming up. Sulgrave. They look good.

Mr Phelan throws us a football and tells us to do our pre-match warm-up in the way we've been trained. As I do my stretching exercises, I look around the Hotshots, wondering how each of us will react to the pressure of this, our biggest moment.

Charlie. No problem there. She could be playing in an FA Cup Final and she'd be the same dependable, rocklike presence.

Roberta. Playing on the wing, she never panics but this is her first big game in goal. She's good enough but she lacks Tara's crazed arrogance. Gerry's right – an early goal against us could be disastrous. If she can just keep a clean sheet for those opening moments, Roberta will be all right.

Stevie. She has never been tested in a big game but the way she took control during Tara's crisis at the fairground suggests that she has a cool head. On the other hand, there's been hardly a single "Oh wow" from her since we arrived at the park. Is this a good sign? Or will she freeze when that whistle goes?

Ellie. In all good teams, there's a player who does the hard work in the middle of the field, supplying the forwards, tackling back in defence – "fetching and carrying", as Gerry calls it. But what if that person has had her head down a lavatory bowl most of the day? If Ellie has to come off, her replacement isn't exactly in the same class as her.

Lisa. Trump card or walking liability? When Lisa's on song there's no one to beat her but, as she proved in the first round, it takes just one distraction to throw her completely. Here she's surrounded by distractions – her mother, teachers from school, Jason and his gang, Patrick. Yes, I find myself worrying about Lisa.

Ellie, Stevie and I are passing the ball between us when I notice a familiar figure making his way from the pitches to our practice area. It's Mr Morley, and he's carrying a sheet of paper in his hand. To my amazement, he walks up to Mr Phelan.

"Oh, no. Now what?" I mutter as the two men stand in earnest conversation. "Morley can't change his mind at this stage about Mr Phelan being here."

"Eve!"

As if Mr Morley has heard what I'm saying, he beckons me over.

"Yes, Mr Morley?"

The headteacher hands me the sheet. "What do you know about this?"

I recognize the handwriting at once – meticulously neat and so small that you almost need a magnifying-glass to read it. It's the writing I've seen on teachers' desks countless times over the past year, usually with the words "See me, please" scrawled in red ink in the margin. There's no mistaking the work of Jamie O'Keeffe. Why the headteacher has brought an essay by Jamie to the Area Finals of the Met Cup remains a mystery until I manage to decipher the microscopically written heading, "HOTSHOTS – The True Story".

"I've never seen this before in my life," I say truthfully.

"Read it, Eve," says Gerry.

With some difficulty, I scan Jamie's essay. He's no Charles Dickens, that's for sure, but the story he has to tell is extraordinary. He explains how Jason's father and Mr Williams are regulars at the same pub as a couple of local policemen, how it was they who sent the information about Gerry's past to the parents and Mr Morley. The main reason why the boys tried to persuade Lisa to join their team, Jamie claims, is that, after one game with them, she wouldn't be allowed to play with the Hotshots in the Met Cup. The boys had goaded Tara into rebellion. They had tried to stop Stevie joining us. "This shows how everybody has been against the Hotshots," Jamie finishes his essay. "The school should be dead proud of what they've done."

I smile. No Charles Dickens – but maybe Sherlock Holmes.

"It sounds like the truth, Mr Morley." I hand the paper back to him. "That's all I know."

"But who wrote it?"

"No idea. None of the Hotshots, that's for sure."

A worries-of-the-world-are-on-my-shoulders frown crosses the headteacher's face. "Your sons and your daughters are beyond your command," he says distantly. "Oh well, I suppose it all worked out for the best. Even if there was this great conspiracy against you, the Hotshots are through to the Area Finals."

Gerry Phelan nods to a corner of the practice area where Tara, in torn-off jeans and a T-shirt, is giving Roberta some practice shots in a goal made of two kit bags. "Not for Tara, it hasn't," he says.

"Yes, well, it wasn't the first time we've had problems with that girl," says Mr Morley with a hint of impatience in his voice.

"Finish your warm-up, Eve," Gerry says to me. "Kick-off's in five minutes."

As I jog back to Lisa and Ellie, I hear Gerry mention the words "car park". Good. At least Mr Morley will know how Tara stood up to her father when it really mattered. But by the time I look back to where the two men were standing, Gerry is there alone. The headteacher, hands sunk deep in his pockets, is walking back towards the pitch.

"Attention, please." The announcement crackles over the loudspeaker system. "Will the Broadhurst Hotshots and Sulgrave Girls, area finalists for the Under 13 Girls section of the Metropolitan Cup, please go to Pitch One."

We huddle around Gerry, a bit like startled sheep. "On you go, girls," he smiles. "Eve, stay close to me during the match – and you, Tara. You're still part of the team, even if you're not playing."

Tara reaches inside her kit bag and brings out a pair of yellow goalkeeping gloves. "Lucky gloves," she smiles, kissing each one flamboyantly before handing them to Roberta. "They never fail."

Roberta takes off her own gloves and throws them in the bag. "Thanks, Tara," she smiles. "I won't let you down."

"Better not," says Tara.

The five Hotshots players run ahead, through the crowd and on to the pitch. As Gerry, Tara and I make our way towards our place next to the entrance, I notice Jamie, standing by himself at the back of the crowd, watching us.

"Good try, Jamie," I whisper as we walk past.

He winks. "You're going to win," he says.

Another surprise awaits us when we reach our places. Jogging beside the Sulgrave Girls at their end of the pitch is a familiar figure in a dark blue tracksuit.

"It's the man who watched us last Saturday," I gasp. "The one who said they were so brilliant. He was their manager all the time."

"Of course," Gerry mutters in a distracted voice. He's frowning as he watches what's happening on the pitch.

Two footballs have been left out for each of the team. Cunningly, Sulgrave have placed our ball beside their goal. In order to fetch it, one of the Hotshots will have to push through the line of running Sulgrave Girls. Uncertain as to what to do, our team stand in a huddle near the centre circle.

"They're psyching us out," Gerry says, almost to himself. He beckons Lisa over to where we're standing. "Take up your positions on the field and look as if you can't wait for the game to start," he says above the growing crowd noise around the ring.

Within seconds, the scene on the pitch has changed. Each of the Hotshots is in position, jogging with quiet concentration. Now it's us who are waiting for them. We're the professionals. Sulgrave Girls, still with their ridiculous gum-chewing manager on the pitch, seem unprepared.

"Nice one, Gerry," says Tara.

Across the ring, Mr Morley stands surrounded by Broadhurst parents. As the referee, a small bald man dressed in black shorts and shirt, strides on to the pitch, there's a roar from the crowd. The Sulgrave manager, with a cocky little thumbs-up sign to his team, jogs towards the entrance to the pitch. Casting a contemptuous look in our direction, he takes up his position on the other side of the gate.

"Good luck, mate," Gerry calls across to him.

The manager glances at us, chewing open-mouthed as he holds Gerry with a cool stare. Then he turns to the pitch. "Put 'em under, girls," he calls out.

"What does that mean?" I ask Gerry.

"It means we're in for a rough, tough game," he says grimly.

Lisa wins the toss and elects to kick off.

The referee checks both goalkeepers are ready. A silence descends on the crowd as he slowly raises the whistle to his lips.

He blows a single shrill blast.

"Yeah." It's a deafening yell from Tara. "Go, Hotshots!"

CHAPTER EIGHT

The Old One Two

For no more than forty or fifty seconds does the game follow the plan Gerry has discussed with us.

Kicking off, Lisa passes the ball to Ellie who calmly kicks back to Roberta in goal to give her a touch of the ball. Roberta rolls the ball out to Stevie who, I'm relieved to see, is playing calmly with no sign of nerves.

Too calmly, perhaps. With an elegant little touch, she tries to pass one of the Sulgrave players by deflecting the ball off the wooden wall, only to find that a second player is there to collect the ball. Under pressure from Lisa, the Sulgrave girl takes an optimistic shot at our goal, which is blocked easily by Charlie.

As if we're back in the park, practising, Charlie lays it off for Ellie who advances down the right wing.

None of this seems to please the Sulgrave manager. "Put her down," he's growling, as if Ellie's some kind of horse. "Let her know you're there – *Annie!*"

I'm just wondering what exactly he means by this when their defender, a powerful girl, each of whose thighs is about the size of my waist, thunders across the pitch towards Ellie.

"Man on, Ellie!" Gerry screams out a warning but it's as if everyone – on the pitch and off – can see what's about to happen except for the target herself. The big girl, Annie, launches herself through the air, clattering Ellie hard into the wall.

The referee blows his whistle shrilly but, as Sulgrave's hitwoman stands up, dusting herself down, Ellie lies moaning on the ground.

Yes, Sulgrave have let her know they were there.

I glare at their manager as the referee gives their player a little lecture about the general inadvisability of trying to kill the opposing players. "Good girl, Annie," he says, as she jogs back to her position, grinning.

Winded, but just about alive, Ellie gets to her feet.

"So much for sportsmanship," mutters Tara.

When play resumes, the Sulgrave plan seems to have worked. Their players may not be as skilful as us but they're big and have been trained how to use their size. While Ellie's still recovering from Big Annie's killer tackle, one of their players dummies past her. Suddenly there are two Sulgrave girls against Charlie in defence. The first draws her, then, as soon as Charlie is committed, passes the ball across the area where a tall girl with short dark hair calmly sidefoots it past Roberta and into the net.

There are roars of approval from Sulgrave's supporters. I glance across to where my parents stand beside Mr Morley. Catching my eye, my mother contributes her most irritating expression – a soppy, sympathetic, shucks-that's-life smile.

I look away, scowling, as Lisa kicks off once more.

Almost immediately, the Hotshots are in trouble again. Ellie seems so shocked by what has happened that she's fallen back in defence beside Charlie.

As the entire Sulgrave team push forward, there's a moment of confusion between the two of them, Charlie loses her balance and puts a foot in the area.

Penalty.

There's silence as Big Annie places the ball on the penalty spot, takes a few steps, then advances with heavy, determined steps. She powers hard and low, giving Roberta no chance of saving it.

2–0. Suddenly I don't care about winning any more. All I'm praying is that we don't get humiliated in front of our parents, the teachers, the boys.

I glance up at Gerry Phelan to find, to my amazement, that he's actually smiling. "We'll be all right," he calls out. "Just play your football, girls."

Something about the way the younger Sulgrave supporters are chanting "Two nil, two nil, two nil" stirs an unprecedented sense of loyalty within Jason and his gang. At first, I can't believe my ears. They're chanting. "Hotshots!" followed by three quick claps.

On the pitch, we're coming alive at last. Suddenly I can see why Gerry's smiling. Sulgrave are relaxing, glancing in the direction of their parents, playing to the gallery.

"Hotshots!" Clap clap clap. Even some of the teachers are joining in. I can hear the shrieks of Mrs Martin above the cheers of the crowd.

If only we can keep calm in the final two minutes of the first half.

We seem to have most of the possession now, Lisa passes to Stevie and sprints towards their goal line, just in time to collect Stevie's perfect return pass.

"The old one two," Gerry mutters beside me.

Lisa shimmies past their defender, looks up and shoots. Their goalkeeper can hardly have seen the shot as it rockets past her.

2–1. The cheers from the boys are deafening.

Tara and I are still leaping up and down, punching the air when my euphoria is destroyed by Mr Phelan.

"Get ready, Eve," he says quietly. "You're going out at half-time."

What? Half a game against those brutes? "But – " My mouth hangs open.

"Don't ask questions." Gerry turns back to the game. "Ellie's too ill to play her normal game. This is what substitutes are for."

I turn with a wide-eyed "Who, me?" look to Tara who smiles.

"Listen, it's 2–1." She puts a consoling hand on my shoulder. "If we lose, it won't be your fault."

The referee blows for half-time.

As the seven of us gather around Gerry Phelan at one end of the pitch, it's obvious that, however bad my footballing skills may be, I'll be more use on the pitch than Ellie. Getting crushed by a rampaging Sulgrave elephant has done nothing for her upset stomach. As she leans forward, staring at the ground, hands on hips, her face is the colour of paper. Painfully, she puts on her sweater and wishes me luck.

I am not a footballer. Other great achievements may

be awaiting me in later life but I'm pretty sure that playing for an England women's XI won't be among them. I reach this conclusion during the second half of the Area Final against Sulgrave Girls.

From the touchline, their players have looked big and clumsy, but that was only when one compared them to Lisa or Stevie. As I rush and buzz about the middle of the pitch like a fly in a jar, I'm lucky to get more than a couple of touches of the ball before one of the opposition players coolly whisks it off me. After a couple of minutes, I've decided that only one tactic matters – get the ball and pass it as quickly as possible to someone better than me, preferably someone on my side. When I don't have the ball, I'll just make a nuisance of myself, harrying and chivvying and generally getting in the way of the Sulgrave players.

But we're playing better now, as if the roar of our supporters has shown us that the game is still within our grasp. Sulgrave on the other hand have lost the arrogant confidence they showed in the first half.

Yet we don't score. The Annie girl is a brilliant defender – strong and quick, she seems to have the measure of Lisa and Stevie. Me, she ignores, confident that on my own I can do nothing.

A minute to go until full-time and it's still 2–1. The Hotshots are heading out of the Met Cup when Sulgrave go for the final, killer goal.

Urged on by their manager, Annie collects the ball in defence. Stevie, Lisa and I hold back expecting her to pass it to one of her forwards, as she has done throughout the game. Charlie moves nearer to her right covering Sulgrave's most dangerous striker.

For a moment, it's as if I'm trapped in a dream. The noise of the crowd fades, everything is in slow motion as I become aware of Gerry Phelan standing like a statue, looking at me but pointing at Annie.

And suddenly I see it. I see what none of the others has seen. *Annie's not going to pass at all!* She's going straight for goal.

No! I hear a scream in my head as I set off across the pitch, my eyes fixed on the ball. The other Hotshots are falling back marking the players to whom they expect Annie to pass. She's five yards from the goal area and travelling fast. Now, too late, the other players see what's about to happen. Annie's just drawing back her right leg to shoot at goal when, like some kind of psycho from a Kung Fu video, I hurl myself through the air feet first.

The world explodes. One moment, Annie's right boot, the ball and I are meeting at the same point in space, the next I'm being crushed under her vast weight as we slide across the grass at a million miles an hour and crash against one of the walls.

Distantly, I'm aware of howls of protest from the Sulgrave players and supporters. Shaking my head I look up to see that the ball has emerged from the tangle of bodies at Lisa's feet. With Annie, their defender, still disentangling herself from me, Lisa coolly advances towards the Sulgrave goal, striking the ball with a stinging right-footed shot.

And misses. There's a groan from our supporters as it hits the sidepost but then suddenly, appearing out of nowhere, Stevie's there. She controls the ball on the rebound and, as calmly as if we're back in the play-ground at Broadhurst, hammers it into the back of the net.

"Equaliser. *Yes!*" I leap up to celebrate the goal, then crumple back down when I put my weight on my right leg. Something weird and uncomfortable seems to have happened to my knee.

From the ground I see the Sulgrave manager striding on to the pitch, protesting to the referee and pointing to where I'm lying in my death throes.

"That was a foul, ref!" he's screaming as the referee waves him away.

Charlie crouches over me and signals to Gerry.

"Ballet." I'm gasping in pain.

"Bally what?" asked Charlie.

"Ballet . . . What about my ballet?"

I lie back on the grass and close my eyes as the pain begins to throb behind my right knee.

There's a matter of seconds to go before full-time, I dimly realize as people gather around me. Then it's extra time. The way I feel, I can hardly walk, let alone play football. The Hotshots will be down to four players.

"Are you all right, darling?"

Oh no. To my horror, my mother's suddenly on the pitch, crouching over me.

"Mum," I groan, the embarrassment making me

forget the pain in my knee for a moment. "Get off the pitch. You're not allowed."

Someone's gently touching my injured leg. It's Gerry.

"Pulled ligament," he says. "It's the injury professional footballers get."

"My ballet exams?" I ask weakly.

"Never mind the ballet." Gerry puts his arms under me and picks me up. "That tackle of yours just kept us in the Metropolitan Cup."

To my amazement, the entire crowd claps as I'm carried off. As Gerry and I reach the gate, the Sulgrave manager looks down at me and nods curtly. "Brave girl," he mutters.

Gerry Phelan passes me to my father, who's standing near by.

"Talk about a kamikaze tackle." Dad smiles, turning away from the pitch where play has restarted.

"I want to stay," I moan. "Got to see the end of the match."

Reluctantly my father puts me down. I lean against the fencing and watch the game on one leg.

Something strange has happened. Although we're now down to four players, the fire seems to have gone out of Sulgrave's play, as if my tackle and Stevie's goal have shown them for the first time that the Hotshots are no pushover.

In those last seconds of normal time, there are no further shots on goal and the crowd seems oddly subdued, as if saving its energy for the five minutes of extra time.

The whistle blows for full-time.

"What are we going to do?" I ask Gerry. "We've only got four players. They're bound to score."

Gerry's staring across the pitch. Following the direction of his eyes, I see that it's Mr Morley whose attention he's trying to attract. When the headteacher looks at him, Gerry points to his left where Tara is standing.

Morley frowns, then looks away. I want to shout across the pitch, remind him of everything that Jamie put in his essay. I want to tell him how Tara stood up to her father to defend Mr Phelan.

But it's not necessary.

The head looks back and, as if he were a Roman emperor or something, gives an imperious little nod.

Yes! I smile in spite of the pain which seems to be spreading up my leg.

Gerry reaches into the kit bag that's lying at his feet and takes out a purple shirt. He hands it to Tara.

"You're right midfield," he says.

"Eh?" Tara's eyes widen in amazement. "Shut up right midfield."

"Never mind your cheekiness," says Gerry. "Get on there and win the match."

Muttering to herself, Tara pulls on the shirt. "But what about these?" she asks, pointing at her cut-off jeans. "Shouldn't I get some shorts on?"

"No time." Gerry opens the gate and signals to the ref that a new player is coming on for extra time.

As Tara jogs on to the pitch there's a buzz of surprise

from the crowd, followed by laughter from some of Sulgrave's supporters.

It's true that, with her wild blonde hair and jeans, she doesn't exactly look the part of a footballing finalist, but then they don't know Tara like we know her.

If they did, they wouldn't be laughing. Tara looks around the crowd, her eyes blazing with anger.

You don't laugh at Tara if you know what's good for you.

As Lisa, Stevie, Charlie and Roberta gather around Tara, smiling and patting her on the back, there's a bellow from the back of the ground.

"My girl!" The voice is unmistakably that of Mr Williams. "They're playing my girl. Come on, you Hotshots."

"Do it, Tara." Ellie, a pale presence standing beside me, mutters to herself.

The teams take up their positions for the last five minutes of play.

Why hasn't Gerry Phelan put Tara in goal?

The thought occurs to me in the first breathless seconds of extra time.

Then I see his plan.

Roberta may not be quite such a good goalkeeper as Tara but she has played well today. Tara, on the other hand, is really fired up for the occasion – just what the Hotshots need on the pitch but not in goal.

Sulgrave Girls have made a substitution too, but the player they have brought on seems to be overcome by the occasion. The more her gum-chewing manager screams at her, the more she stumbles about ineffectively in midfield.

For the first two minutes of extra time, we're on the attack but nothing, it seems, can get past Annie, the giant defender, or their goalkeeper.

"What happens if it's still two all at full-time?" Ellie asks Mr Phelan.

"Penalties."

"We'll need to change keepers then," I say. "Tara's great at saving penalties."

The manager smiles thinly. "Not allowed," he says, his eyes following the game as he speaks. "That was my gamble. We've got to win in extra time. If it goes to penalties, we have real problems."

By now there are tired players on both sides but, with all four Sulgrave players back in defence, no one seems likely to break the deadlock. That is until, with a penalty shoot-out only a minute and a half away, their goalkeeper saves a shot from Stevie and takes our players by surprise by rolling the ball straight up the pitch for their striker to pursue.

For once in her life, Charlie is out of position, stranded on the halfway line as the ball streaks past her with the Sulgrave striker in pursuit. Suddenly the Sulgrave girl has only Roberta to beat to score the winning goal.

Without a moment's hesitation, Roberta takes in the situation at a glance. She sprints out of her area towards the ball. It's a crazy gamble. The Sulgrave player's a couple of yards away from the ball – if she reaches it before Roberta, we've lost. She'll have an open goal in front of her.

"No," whispers Gerry beside me.

"Oh, Roberta," Ellie groans.

Maybe it's the surprise of seeing our goalkeeper way out of her area. Perhaps Roberta is faster than any of us realize. Either way, she reaches the ball first – and then pulls out her biggest surprise of all.

The simplest, the most logical, the *only* thing to do is to play for safety, to blast the ball off the pitch. Roberta, for reasons I will never understand, decides not to do this. Instead she deploys our ultimate, our secret weapon, the bane of Miss Wilson's life – her deadly left foot.

From all around us, there seems to be a gasp as Roberta's foot makes contact with the ball. Flying with the speed of a rocket, it finds its way through all the players in front of her except one – Big Annie. Desperately, the Sulgrave defender thrusts her size ten trainers at the ball, changing its direction away from the centre of the goal – and into the corner of the net.

The noise is so loud, and the throbbing behind my right knee so insistent, that I remember little after that. During the last minute of the game, Sulgrave throw all their players forward while Tara, Stevie and Lisa fall back to defend Roberta's goal beside Charlie.

It's the longest minute of my life.

When at last it ends with that welcome blast of the whistle, I find myself embracing Ellie, my dad, Gerry. I even manage to hop on to the pitch to hug the players. On the other side of the pitch, Jason and his gang are jubilantly punching the air, watched with faint, smiling disapproval by Mr Morley and the parents.

Gerry shakes the Sulgrave manager's hand and congratulates their players.

As he makes his way towards the pitch to greet his team, one of the policemen smiles at him warmly, then pats him lightly on the back.

CHAPTER NINE

Love and Football

The team photograph, taken at that moment of triumph, is on the cork board in front of my desk. It's one of those rare pictures where all the people in it seem to be happy in their own way, where no one's eyes are shut. There's a sort of balance to the scene, a unity as if we're some kind of complicated circus act caught as we took the applause just before falling apart.

Later – seconds later, it seems to me now – the act would topple, the magic of that perfect moment would fade. Yet even now, back in the real world of rivalries, and problems of home and school, each of us has kept a memory of the time when, in spite of everything the world and Mr Morley could throw at us, we stuck together and won through.

Every picture tells a story. This one tells several.

In the front row of the team shot, Stevie is kneeling down, her arm (incredibly) hanging around Lisa's shoulders. Would you believe that this was the beginning of a beautiful friendship? Suddenly the two biggest egos in the school are going around like the Together

148

Twins, off to the cinema, kicking a ball about in the park, talking for hours and hours about clothes and boys.

Right now, as we prepare to take the Hotshots to Wembley for the grand final of the Cup, Lisa's home life has suddenly become too strange even for her. And who does she turn to? Stevie Rostand.

In the photograph, Ellie's staring into space with an invalid's stare while, behind her, Roberta chats to someone off camera. At the centre of the back row, Tara and Charlie stand like a couple of sentries, virtually obscuring an insignificant figure who's standing between them. This, with the help of a powerful magnifying glass, you would discover to be me.

Charlie has a normal, smile-for-the-cameras grin on her face but there's something defiant and closed off about Tara's smile. It's the sort of expression people put on when posing for police mugshots.

Tara, you may not be surprised to hear, doesn't exactly believe in those happy-ever-after endings. Within a week of our victory, she's back on detention for fighting with Jason in the playground. All this summer she's been in trouble with her parents, with the school and then, finally, with our friends the police.

"It was success with the Hotshots that did it," Ellie says to me the other day. "Success turned Tara's brain."

"Brain?" I have to laugh. "What brain?"

And it's not just Tara who makes sure that the Hotshots' connection with the Metropolitan Police lasts through the summer months. Standing slightly aside from the team in the picture on my wall is Jamie

O'Keeffe, whom Gerry Phelan has insisted should be part of the team photo.

A few weeks later Jamie's pale face, smiling warily, will appear in the local papers once more but in an unhappier context. But that's another story.

Gerry Phelan's luckier. Beside the team photograph, where the manager stands beside his team wearing the professional public smile he learnt during his glory days as a footballer, there's a cutting from the *Independent*. The headline reads "FORGOTTEN FOOTBALL HERO IN SENSATIONAL 'CUP' WIN!"

It's one of those jokey little pieces that journalists like to write when there's nothing much else to report.

Gerry Phelan, the controversial Fulham star of the seventies, made a surprise return to cup football last week – as manager of a local schoolgirls' team. Phelan, who faded from the public eye after scoring a two-year jail sentence for receiving stolen goods in 1981, coached the under 13 girls' team from his local school Broadhurst Junior to a famous victory in the south-west Area Final of the Metropolitan Cup. By a happy irony, the cup is organized by Phelan's old friends the Metropolitan Police.

Gerry Phelan's capacity for surprise, so much a feature of his Fulham days, is clearly still intact – the bizarre winning goal from the Broadhurst Hotshots was scored by their own goalkeeper. Their 3–2 win will take Gerry Phelan's team back to his favourite stamping-ground, Wembley Stadium, for the overall finals in the autumn. The Metropolitan Police spokes-

> *man refused to comment on the success of ex-jailbird*
> *Gerry and his Hotshots.*

Very hilarious. Very sexist.

But Gerry has the last laugh. A couple of weeks later, he's contacted by his old club Fulham. They're looking for a coach for their youth team. Would Gerry be interested?

Now he's back in work, doing the job he loves best. That perhaps has been the best part of the Hotshots' success.

But what if we hadn't won? What if Roberta's moment of madness had resulted not in a "bizarre" goal for us but had given victory to Sulgrave?

In the background to the team photograph, I can see the broad, slightly hunched shoulders of Mr Morley. As we're exulting in our win and posing for the cameras, I notice the headteacher going over to the Sulgrave Girls, some of whom are crying. He pats them on the back and shakes their hands. He speaks to their manager who, to judge from Mr Morley's stunned smile, is not exactly being sporting in defeat.

Later, I find myself thinking back to that morning when Mr Morley walked into our class and announced his team of nerdbrains that would represent the school in the Metropolitan Cup. We outflanked him, laughed at his idea that there was more to competing than just winning at all costs.

Now I'm not so sure.

A fist, clenched, punching the air, can be seen in the top right-hand corner of the photograph.

It belongs, I suppose, to Mr Williams – after the final whistle, he goes around behaving as if his daughter had beaten Sulgrave single-handed.

Now that we were "winners", as he calls us, Tara's dad starts taking a closer interest in the Hotshots. The news of Mr Phelan's job with Fulham gives him his chance. Who will manage the Hotshots now? Who will take them on the glory trail to the Met Final at Wembley in November?

Step forward, Mr Williams.

Wembley with Tara's dad? We'll see about that.

Look closer at the shrimp in the back row. The pain in my knee is fading now. Before I drive home, a First Aid woman looks at me and diagnoses a pulled muscle – nothing serious but my ballet exam, just as I thought, will have to wait, big tragedy.

But I'm not looking at my mum and dad when the photographer presses the button. My eyes are turned towards someone who unmistakably is smiling at me, eyes in full smoulder mode.

Patrick.

Patrick? Looking at me?

Surely not.

I glance down at Lisa. Phew. If she weren't too busy posing for the camera to notice what was happening, the picture in the local paper might have shown two members of the victorious Hotshots team scratching each other's eyes out.

I look back. Patrick is still smiling at me. He lifts a thumb in a lazy gesture of congratulation. My one good leg almost gives way. I smile back, shrugging modestly. A shrimp in love.

"I'm not sure I can stand the fame," Tara's saying. Near where Patrick is standing, Lisa's mother is moving towards us as if drawn towards the camera by a giant magnet.

The photographer fusses about with the camera. Through a fixed smile, Ellie mutters, "If he doesn't get his act together, he'll be just in time to catch me throwing up again."

"Like, this is just so weird," says Stevie, as if she's talking to herself. "This is the weirdest football team ever ever *ever*."

And suddenly we're all laughing again – weird we may be but together we've won.

Cut to the future. It's soon time for the grand final at Wembley and the usual Hotshot confusion has returned.

Will we manage to stay together that long? What will Lisa say when she discovers that Patrick is more interested in the substitute than the star striker? In the great battle of love and football, who will be the winner? Does winning matter that much anyway?

The answer, my friend, as Mr Morley would say, is blowing in the wind.